For the Least of These

MYSTERY
and the
MINISTER'S
WIFE®

For the Least of These

CHARLOTTE CARTER

GUIDEPOSTS
New York, New York

www.guideposts.com
(800) 431-2344
Guideposts Books & Inspirational Media

Cover design by Dugan Design Group
Cover illustration by Dan Brown
Interior design by Cris Kossow
Typeset by Nancy Tardi
Printed in the United States of America

Chapter One

A warm spring afternoon, and the hum of honeybees lured Kate Hanlon to her backyard. She'd always enjoyed gardening at her home in San Antonio, but since her husband, Paul, had been called to pastor Faith Briar Church in Copper Mill, Tennessee, her days had been so busy, she rarely found the time.

Whoever claimed that the pace of life in a small town was slower than it was in the city had never lived in Copper Mill.

But with every new challenge, both she and Paul thanked the Lord for leading them here. They'd made new friends who had deepened and enriched their lives, and they'd come to think of Copper Mill as their home.

Dressed in an old T-shirt and jeans, with gardening gloves, a trowel, clippers, a weeding knife, and a rake in hand, Kate marched to the flower bed at the back of her small yard. Weeds had invaded the fertile patch of dark black Tennessee soil. Today she'd battle the advance of unwanted Indian grass and broomsedge and tame the indigo bush that had gone to stalk from neglect.

To lay out what she hoped to accomplish, she'd drawn a diagram of the yard, including the large maple tree that shaded the house in summer. She planned to landscape with flowers and plants native to Tennessee—azaleas and rhododendrons would mark the shady corners of the yard. Blue phlox, sunflowers, and asters would provide a backdrop along the split-rail fence for bedding plants, such as petunias. She'd plant ferns in a perpetually shady area by the house, and she'd reserve one sunny spot for her beloved Texas bluebonnets.

Once the flower beds were under control, she'd deal with restoring the lawn. She hoped by late summer she'd be able to host an outdoor tea for the church ladies back here.

Working on her knees, she snipped back gangly indigo-bush branches and yanked up wayward grass by the roots. Beneath her straw gardening hat, beads of sweat formed and crept down her neck. She wiped her forehead with the back of her gloved hand. The leaves of the dogwood tree on the wooded hillside behind her yard rustled, but the cooling breeze failed to reach her.

If Paul hadn't been so busy with his pastoral duties, she would have asked for his help.

Sitting back on her haunches, she took a deep breath and said a brief prayer. Perhaps she'd bitten off more than her fifty-seven-year-old body could—

"Afternoon, ma'am."

Startled by the voice behind her, Kate lost her balance and plopped down on her rear end.

She turned to see a girl of about thirteen standing in her

yard. Her stringy blonde hair reached below the collar of her black T-shirt. There were ragged holes in both knees of her jeans. Somehow Kate didn't think the holes were a youthful fashion statement, but rather a sign of hard use.

"Hello, yourself." Kate smiled while shifting to a more comfortable position.

"I didn't mean to scare you." The girl's accent carried the soft lilt of one born and bred in Appalachian country.

"It's all right. I was lost in thought and didn't hear you coming." She studied the youngster and wondered about her solemn expression. "Were you looking for Pastor Paul?"

The girl scuffed the toe of her sneaker in the grass, a shoe that looked as worn as her jeans.

"Not really, ma'am. I saw you workin' out here and thought maybe you could use some help." She looked up from the study of her shoes, her eyes pleading. "I'm a real hard worker, ma'am."

"Oh, I'm sure you are." Kate was about to thank her for her offer and send her away, but another thought skittered through her brain. *Lord, did you send this girl in answer to my prayer or hers?*

"You're looking for a job?" Kate asked.

The girl's head bobbed up and down. "I'm stronger than I look, ma'am. You don't have to pay me much, and I'll do anything that needs doing."

"Well . . ." Kate got to her feet, her arthritic knee giving a twinge in the process. "I'm sure we'll be able to work something out." Removing her glove, she extended her hand. "I'm Kate Hanlon, the pastor's wife."

A glimmer of hope sparked in the girl's blue eyes. "Megan Maddock, ma'am." She gave Kate's hand two hearty pumps. "I live out Smoky Mountain Hollow way."

Kate had lived in Copper Mill long enough to know that some residents of the nearby hollows lived much as people had at the turn of the twentieth century and were still mired in poverty. She'd seen houses that were little more than shacks and families living in old, run-down trailers. She feared the Maddock family was one of those, and her heart went out to the girl.

"Do you go to school, Megan?"

"Sure do, ma'am. Seventh grade at Copper Mill Elementary School. Got me a prize last year for paintin' the best safety poster for school."

"Congratulations." Tickled by the girl's pride in her accomplishment, Kate had to restrain an amused grin. "Then you're just looking for work after school, right?"

"Uh, yes, ma'am. I gotta be . . . My ma wants me home by dark."

"Good for her." Kate looked at the remaining flower beds that needed to be cleared of weeds. "We'd better get started then."

They settled into the task, for the most part in companionable silence. Young Megan worked like a junior-sized steam shovel, digging out every encroaching root she could find in the flower bed and tossing it on the growing pile of discarded weeds. Kate couldn't recall her own children working that hard in the yard, though to their credit, they'd done their chores without complaint. Usually.

"Were you born here in Copper Mill?" Kate asked.

"No, ma'am."

"How long have you lived here?"

Megan dug hard around a root-ball of grass. "A few years."

The girl certainly wasn't a chatterbox. In fact, she didn't seem very forthcoming in her answers, and Kate wondered why. Paul often reminded Kate that she'd find a mystery even where there wasn't one, that she saw riddles that needed to be solved. Perhaps he was right. But her intuition was telling her something different.

After about an hour, Kate knew she needed a break and imagined that Megan did too.

"I think I'll make a pitcher of lemonade. I've got some chocolate-chip cookies too. Would you like some, Megan?"

The girl's eyes widened, and the very first smile she'd bestowed on Kate teased at the corners of Megan's lips.

"That'd be real nice, ma'am."

Kate entered the house, then splashed some water on her face and ran a comb through her strawberry-blonde hair, which did little to repair the damage that had been done by wearing a hat.

It took only a few minutes to mix up the lemonade and place a few cookies on a plate. Using a tray, she carried the refreshments and two glasses outside. Megan was still hard at work.

"Come sit in the shade and cool off while you have your snack." She placed the tray on the black wrought-iron patio table and sat down in one of the two matching chairs, then filled the two glasses with lemonade.

Megan didn't need a second invitation. Sweat dampened

her T-shirt, which clung to her body as she took the chair opposite Kate. She noticed how truly thin Megan was as the girl consumed the entire glass of lemonade without taking a breath. That worried her.

"Do you have brothers and sisters?" Kate slid the plate of cookies toward her.

"Yes, ma'am. One of each. I'm the oldest." Delicately, she selected a cookie and nibbled a bite. She grinned. "These are good."

"Help yourself to more if you'd like. I have plenty inside."

Megan eyed the three remaining cookies. Then, as carefully as she'd chosen the first one, she placed the cookies in a paper napkin and wrapped them up. Then she chugged down the second glass of lemonade Kate had poured for her.

"Thanks for the cookies and lemonade, ma'am. I'll get back to work now."

Megan placed her precious bundle of cookies on the grass next to where she was working and dove back into the task at hand.

She was going to share those cookies with her siblings, Kate realized and smiled. Sweet child. But Megan troubled Kate too. She seemed so needy, her eyes pleading when she'd asked for a job, and so anxious to please.

When it came time to pay her, Kate gave Megan a couple of extra dollars for her efforts beyond the hourly rate they'd agreed upon.

With a look of delight, Megan stuffed the money into her pocket. "I'll be back tomorrow right after school, ma'am, if that's okay with you."

"Perfect. We still have lots of work to do."

As the girl jogged off down the road, Kate made a mental note to call on Megan and her family. She sensed they needed more help than a few extra dollars and a handful of cookies.

"THERE'S NOTHING BETTER than to come home after a long day to my beautiful wife, who just happens to be fixing dinner," Paul said as he slipped up behind Kate in the kitchen. She was putting together a ham, apple, and pecan salad at the counter when Paul slid his arms around her waist and nuzzled a kiss to her neck.

"*Hmm*," she said with a smile. "I'll have you know, your wife has put in a pretty hard day of work herself."

She tilted her head to kiss him on the lips. It continued to amaze her that after nearly thirty years of marriage, she always felt a tingle of pleasure when Paul kissed her.

He plucked a candied pecan from the salad and popped it in his mouth. "Hard at work making more stained-glass sun catchers?"

"Not today. I've started on the backyard. I'm determined to have a flowering garden by late summer, so I can invite the ladies to tea."

"That's a pretty big project to take on by yourself." Without being asked, Paul got out silverware and place mats and carried them to the oak table on the other side of the kitchen counter. "I'll try to find some time this week to help, but my schedule's pretty full."

Though the kitchen was far smaller than Kate would have preferred, and the cupboards were a faded yellow, she had added her own touches, including a fine collection of Mauviel copperware, which hung on a rack from the ceiling.

"Not to worry," she said. "I've hired a helper."

Paul's head snapped up from his task of setting the table. "Hired?"

"She's a hard worker." Kate slipped a pan of whole-wheat rolls into the oven to heat.

"Katie, honey, I'm not sure we can afford—"

"She works cheap," she said with a teasing glint in her eyes. "And she's only thirteen years old."

Paul's concerned expression evaporated, and he smiled. "A neighborhood youngster?"

"Actually, no. She lives in the hollows, and I'm worried about her and her family." Kate handed him two plates and filled their glasses with water as she told him about Megan Maddock.

"It does sound like the girl's family could use the extra money," Paul said.

"That's what I thought too." She slid the salad bowl across the counter for Paul. "We had some leftover ham from Sunday's supper that I wanted to use up."

"Any dish that has your candied pecans in it is fine with me."

Carrying the plate of warm rolls to the dining area, Kate took her seat at the oak table that had been a part of their lives almost from the beginning. She remembered their children—Andrew, Melissa, and Rebecca—doing their homework at the table and cherished the memories of the family meals they'd all shared together.

Though Paul's hair was now salt-and-pepper gray, to Kate, he was still the young, handsome assistant minister who had swept her off her feet so many years ago in San Antonio. Now they were in Tennessee with a far smaller congregation than the one he'd ministered to in Texas, but no less happy than they'd been there.

Paul lowered his head to say grace, and Kate added a silent prayer for Megan's family.

As they ate, Kate asked Paul about his day.

"An older woman in Pine Ridge had a bad fall last night, and it looks like she'll need hip surgery. I spent most of the afternoon trying to locate her daughter, who lives in Atlanta now."

"It's so hard when your children move away."

"Hard on everybody." He buttered his roll and took a bite. "I know our kids miss us."

"At least we talk to them often, but it's still hard to have them so far away. And the grandchildren."

He nodded, agreeing with her sentiment. "Also, Saturday morning I'm meeting with Sam Gorman and some of the other merchants to finalize plans for Old Timer's Day on the Town Green. We've only got three weeks to go until the event."

Samuel Gorman, owner of the local Mercantile as well as longtime church organist and choir director, had become one of Paul's closest friend in Copper Mill.

"There'll be old-fashioned games for the children," Paul continued. "Hoop rolling and three-legged races, kite flying, and prizes for the best-decorated kites."

"Sounds like a lot of fun."

"Steve Smith is going to organize a booth to sell Appalachian crafts. You think he'll want to display some of your stained-glass pieces?"

"I'll ask him, although stained glass isn't a typical Appalachian craft."

"I'm sure he'll stretch the point for you."

Steve had been kind enough to take some of her stained glass on consignment at his shop, Smith Street Gifts. She'd been more than pleased with the number of pieces that had sold so far.

"There'll be food booths too," Paul said. "I was thinking the church ladies might want to have a bake sale to raise money for the Faith Freezer Program."

"I'm sure they'll want to. We're always running short of donations. We do have a lot of excellent cooks in the congregation."

"But you're the best," he said, scooping up another forkful of salad.

Kate smiled. "We're starting a springtime women's Bible-study group. I'll ask if the women in the group would be willing to provide some baked goods for the booth and staff it too."

"Perfect. A food booth could be another way to keep Faith Briar Church visible in the community. Could even attract new members."

She raised a mocking brow. "You are a clever man, Reverend Hanlon."

He gave her a smug look. "Of course. That's why you married me, isn't it?"

She laughed out loud and gently smacked the back of her

hand against his arm. She couldn't imagine her life without the man she loved so deeply. *Thank you, Lord, for bringing us together*.

On a more serious note, Kate's thoughts turned to Megan and the troubling feeling that the child needed more help than a few extra dollars could provide.

Chapter Two

The next morning, Kate had spent just a few minutes contemplating the day's Scripture reading when the doorbell rang.

"Early for a visitor," she murmured, setting her Bible aside. She'd been sitting in her rocking chair, where she also had a view of the backyard through the sliding-glass door. Of course, she'd have a much clearer view of the yard if the milky calcium deposits on the doors hadn't obscured it.

Grimacing, she crossed the room to the front door. The only person she knew who'd come calling so early in the morning was Renee Lambert, and the moment she opened the door, she caught a whiff of Estée Lauder's Youth-Dew, Renee's trademark perfume.

"Good morning, Renee. You're up early this morning."

On a river of scent, the older woman swept past Kate into the living room. Dressed in her usual bright print warm-up suit, every strand of her dyed blonde hair was perfectly in place, and her high-heeled stilettos clicked on the slate entry. Kisses peered out from a designer tote that swung from Renee's arm.

"Kate, I need a cup of tea." She whirled to face Kate, who had dutifully followed her into the living room.

"Is something wrong?" Kate asked.

"Wrong?" In practically a swoon, Renee collapsed onto the love seat. "Besides the fact that my mother accused me of spoiling Little Umpkins—which is preposterous— everything's fine." She held the dog up to her face and made little kissing noises. "What a mean thing to say about you, Snuggle Umpkins."

Kate valiantly tried not to roll her eyes. "I'll put on some water."

"Loose-leaf Earl Grey, as always, dear. Three sugar cubes, please. And a little half-and-half, warmed, if you don't mind."

Kate knew the routine all too well. "It'll just take a minute."

In the kitchen, she pulled out one of her decorative teapots and two matching cups from the cupboard. Renee was sometimes difficult to deal with, but the woman had a good heart and Kate had become fond of her in spite of her flair for the melodramatic.

Kate preheated the teapot with hot tap water and found the tin of Earl Grey, which she kept on hand for just such an occasion.

When everything was ready, she carried a tray into the living room and set it on an end table beside Renee.

Kisses yipped a friendly greeting from his tote.

"Hello, Kisses," Kate said. "How are you today?"

"Upset, the poor itty-bitty thing. Mother hurt my Little Umpkins' feelings." Renee's mother, Caroline Beauregard Johnston, lived with her, and confrontation between the two strong-willed women occurred with some frequency.

Kate poured the tea and let Renee add her own cream and sugar.

Renee exhaled loudly. "Mother isn't always the easiest person to live with, you know . . . and anyway, I was hoping . . ." Renee sipped her tea, then sighed in satisfaction. "Of course, I hate to impose . . ."

Kate knew very well that Renee was about to impose, reluctant or not.

"Would you mind terribly driving my mother to Green Acres in Pine Ridge? I simply haven't the time or patience to take her to visit her friends today. Besides, Mother insists on riding in the front seat of my car, and you know that's where Kisses likes to sit."

Kate closed her eyes and took a deep breath. "Of course . . . I completely understand." She took a sip of her own tea. At the moment, she would have preferred a strong cup of coffee.

"You are my dearest friend, Kate. Isn't she, Umpkins?" Renee gazed into the tote and made more kissing noises.

Paul stepped out of the bedroom dressed in his running shorts, a T-shirt stenciled with a logo from a 5K run, and his warm-up jacket.

"Good morning, Renee. I thought I heard you out here."

Renee fluttered her French-manicured fingers at him. "I was just asking your dear wife if she'd take Mother to Green Acres for a visit today."

Kate forced a smile. "Renee and her mother need a little time-out."

Paul shot Kate a surprised look. He knew Kate had a full schedule.

"Sometimes Mother gets lonely for her friends," Renee added.

And sometimes Renee took advantage of her friendships, Kate thought. "I have to check in with the volunteers at Faith Freezer today." She suppressed a sigh of defeat.

The Faith Freezer Program had been her special church project to provide food for those who were homebound or in need. She'd planned to spend the whole morning there taking an inventory of what was on hand and then return to her gardening.

"After that," Kate went on, "I'll pick up your mother and drive her to Green Acres. She can have lunch there."

"Perfect!" Renee popped to her feet. Kisses' tote took a wild swing, and he dropped down out of sight inside the bag. "I'll let Mother know you're coming. You'll bring her back before dinner, won't you?"

"I can do that," Paul offered. "I have to see John Sharpe about the church's insurance coverage this afternoon. I can run on down to Green Acres after that."

Kate met her husband's gaze, sending him a quick *thank-you.*

"Then it's all arranged." High heels clicking, Renee bustled to the front door. "Thanks for the tea. I do love a good pick-me-up in the morning."

Kate took Paul's hand, and they followed Renee to the door, then closed it behind her.

"I'm guessing you weren't eager to volunteer to take Caroline to Green Acres," Paul said after Renee left.

"That would be a good guess."

He kissed her lightly. "That's why I love you, Katie. You don't let a little thing like being imposed upon bother you."

She leaned her forehead against his shoulder and chuckled. "Go for your run, dear. I'll just quietly stand here banging my head against the wall till it stops hurting."

Laughing, he kissed her again before heading out the door for his morning jog.

ON A PARTIALLY WOODED LOT between the parsonage and Faith Briar Church, the Faith Freezer Program occupied a small white clapboard house with black shutters.

Kate found Dot Bagley and Martha Sinclair working in the kitchen. While certainly not spacious, it was large enough to cook hot meals.

"Something smells good," Kate said, smiling at the two regular Faith Freezer volunteers.

Dot looked up from spreading mayonnaise on slices of bread. "Martha's making her creamed chicken-and-noodle casserole. It's tasty enough to make an old lady want to dance again."

"Oh, hush." A faint blush colored Martha's cheeks.

Kate chuckled. "Do either of you know the Maddock family that lives in the hollows?"

Dot and Martha had both lived in the community so long, she imagined they knew everyone for miles in all directions. They also happened to be fruit-bearing branches on the Copper Mill grapevine.

Dot shook her head. "Most of the hollow folks stick to themselves."

She watched as Martha served up individual portions of the casserole in aluminum dishes. "How's our inventory doing?"

"We've got plenty of bread," Martha said. "The bakery in Pine Ridge gave us a bunch of day-old loaves and some rolls too. I put them in the freezer till we need them."

"That's good."

Kate jotted down a list of supplies they needed—canned tomatoes, butter, olive oil, basil, and noodles—and tucked it in her pocket. The congregation at Faith Briar Church contributed to the Faith Freezer budget, but the money was still tight. She'd have to spend it very carefully if they were going to make it to the end of the month.

The proceeds from a bake sale would be most welcome.

BY THE TIME Kate dropped off Caroline Johnston at Green Acres, picked up supplies for the Faith Freezer, stopped to pick up her dry cleaning, and fixed herself a bite to eat, it was almost midafternoon.

She changed into her old grubbies and went out to the

garden. The weeds that she and Megan hadn't gotten to the day before appeared to have spread again overnight.

With a groan, she sank to her knees and got to work. It wasn't long before Megan appeared, giving Kate a shy smile.

"Afternoon, Miz Hanlon."

"Good afternoon to you too, Megan. Ready to get to work?"

"Yes, ma'am." The girl quickly picked up the weeding knife and a short claw tool, then knelt a few feet from Kate.

"How was school today?" Kate asked.

"Fine, I guess."

"You're in seventh grade, right?"

"Yes, ma'am." Megan grunted as she pulled on a particularly tenacious clump of Indian grass.

"I remember my seventh-grade English teacher, Miss Marsh. She was wonderful. What's your favorite class?"

"Art. I'm real good at that."

"Is your mother artistic too?"

"Some, I guess."

Again, Kate caught a hint of evasiveness. "Does your mother work in town?"

For several moments, Megan continued to dig up the root she was after before she answered. "Ma's been sick lately."

"I'm sorry to hear that." Kate sensed that Megan didn't want to talk about her mother. Perhaps she considered Kate's questions as prying. A lot of families insisted on maintaining their privacy. Kate could respect that, despite her curiosity about the girl and the mystery about her family.

The conversation went a little better when Kate switched

to the topic of music, although she had to admit she hadn't heard of most of the groups that Megan enjoyed listening to.

Clearly, with her own children grown and off on their own, Kate was out of touch with teenage preferences in musical styles that constantly evolved.

But later, when Kate paid Megan the few dollars she'd earned for her hard work, Kate was confident the girl wouldn't be spending any of the money on music CDs or iPod downloads. Somehow she knew that the cash would go straight toward helping provide for her family.

The next morning, Saturday, Kate borrowed Paul's pickup truck to drive to Jenkins Nursery near Pine Ridge. She wanted to work some soil supplement into the flower beds and buy the first of the plants she needed. Paul could use her Honda Accord to get to his Old Timer's Day planning meeting with Sam.

The two-lane highway to Pine Ridge cut through wooded areas of hemlock, ash, sugar maple, and beech, all bright with new growth. Through the branches, Kate caught an occasional glimpse of a log cabin or a more modern two-story house with a wisp of smoke coming out its chimney. Along the grassy shoulder of the road, wildflowers waved in the breeze created by passing vehicles.

The good Lord had outdone himself when it came to springtime in Tennessee.

Unfortunately, she wasn't the only one who had decided today was a good day to spruce up the garden. The parking lot at the nursery was crowded. Inside, people milled about, and the line at the cash register was a mile long.

The Help Wanted signs on the door and behind the counter made it all the more evident that Floyd Jenkins, the owner, needed to hire more employees.

After paying at the cash register, Kate wrestled two bags of soil amendment, a pair of pink azaleas, and two large rhododendron bushes into the rear of the truck.

Eager to get back to her gardening, Kate hurried home. When she arrived, she discovered that Megan was already hard at work. Only this time the girl had brought along two younger versions of herself.

Chapter Three

Megan quickly rose to her feet when she saw Kate. "Your husband said it'd be okay if my brother and sister helped me."

Kate glanced at the younger children, who looked worried that they'd be sent away. The boy's shaggy blond hair kept falling in front of his eyes, and the girl had used a rubber band to tie hers back in a ponytail. Megan had done the same, except her ponytail was sticking out through the back of a baseball cap.

"Of course they can help," Kate said. "God blesses all who work with their hands."

"He does?" Megan asked.

"Absolutely. It pretty much says so in the Bible."

Megan's forehead furrowed into a frown. "We don't know much about God or the Bible or anything like that."

Lord, you really knew what you were doing when you sent these youngsters to me.

Squatting down next to Megan's younger sister, Kate asked, "What's your name?"

"I'm Gwen. This is my brother, Becker. Everybody calls him Beck."

"Well, I'm glad to meet you, Gwen." Kate shook the young girl's hand, then turned to her brother and did the same. "And Beck too. My only problem is I don't think I can afford to pay all of you what I'm paying your sister."

"That's okay," Gwen said. "We just didn't want to stay home alone all day."

With a mental jolt, Kate registered the *alone* part of Gwen's response and wondered if her mother's health had improved . . . or taken a turn for the worse. And where was their father?

"You could pay us in cookies," Beck said solemnly, his blue eyes squinting in the bright sunlight.

"Hush, Beck!" his big sister admonished him. "Miz Hanlon doesn't have to pay you at all."

Suppressing a smile, Kate said, "You know, Beck, I think I could afford some cookies. If you work really, really hard."

The boy's eyes widened with excitement. "Yes, ma'am. I'll work my hardest ever. I promise."

"Then we have a deal." Kate stood up. "Who wants to help me carry the plants I bought at the nursery? They're in the back of the truck."

With obvious enthusiasm, the two younger children raced to the front of the house where the truck was parked.

Megan seemed less excited about the prospect of fetching and carrying. "You don't have to give us cookies, ma'am. Whatever you want to pay me is plenty."

Because she sensed the gesture wouldn't be welcomed,

Kate resisted the urge to wrap her arms around Megan's slender shoulders and hug her.

"I know. But I love to bake, and the truth is, both my husband and I have been gaining some weight lately. If you three eat up some of the cookies I've made, you'll save us from the temptation of eating them ourselves."

Looking skeptical, Megan lifted her shoulders in a shrug.

"Come with me," Kate said. "I've got a couple of bags of soil amendment in the truck that are too heavy for me or your brother and sister to carry. I'll need your help."

Gwen and Beck had climbed into the bed of the truck. Kate lowered the tailgate.

"Think you can each handle one of the potted plants? They're pretty heavy," Kate warned.

"I'm real strong," Beck insisted.

"So am I," Gwen argued. "That's 'cuz I'm older than you."

"Doesn't matter, 'cuz I'm a boy, and boys are the strongest."

"Quit bickering," Megan ordered her siblings. "Miz Hanlon doesn't want to hear you two fussin' all the time."

Helping the two younger children from the truck, Kate made sure they had a firm grip on their assigned plants before they headed for the backyard. Then she and Megan each hefted a rhododendron and followed them.

"We've got a lot of these bushes growing around our place," Megan said.

"Do you help your mother with her gardening?"

Megan didn't answer the question directly. "Nobody planted 'em. They just grow natural all on their own."

"This is great country for wild rhododendrons. A little

later in the year, the hills will be covered with their colors. A regular painter's pallet of pink and white."

For the moment, Kate had the youngsters set the plants aside to resume their weed pulling while she and Megan hauled the soil amendment to the backyard.

The younger children weren't quite as careful about getting all the roots as Megan, but their determination made up for what they lacked in skill.

Working next to Beck, Kate asked, "How's your mother been feeling, Beck?"

The boy angled a surreptitious look toward his older sister. "Ma's been sick."

"I'm sorry to hear that. I hope she gets to feeling better soon."

"Me too," the boy mumbled.

Something wasn't quite right about the way the children talked about their mother. Was she ill? Or was something else the matter?

"Does your father help take care of her?" Kate asked.

"Nope." The boy yanked extra hard on a handful of grass. "He's in jail."

That news took a moment to settle in. "What for?"

"He kilt somebody."

"Becker!" Megan said. "You talk too much. She doesn't want to hear about our business. Keep your mouth zipped, okay?"

Beck ducked his head, averting his eyes from Kate. "Ma says we're not s'posed to talk about it 'cuz we might get kilt too," he said under his breath.

Nerves tingling, Kate asked, "Are you in danger?"

"Beck! What'd I just tell you?" Grabbing Beck by the arm, Megan half hauled him to a spot on the other side of where she was working. "Don't mind him, Miz Hanlon. Beck likes to make up stuff."

The boy had said his father had killed someone so casually, it didn't sound like make-believe to Kate. What a terrible burden for these children to carry, if it was true.

That was something she'd have to investigate for the safety of the children. Who were the Maddocks, and where did they come from?

By noon, one flower bed had been stripped of weeds. Kate put the children to work mixing in the soil amendment while she went inside to fix sandwiches and lemonade for their lunch.

When she had everything ready, she invited the children inside to wash up and carried the tray outside to the patio table. A warbler was singing from the trees beyond the back fence, and somewhere a gray squirrel chattered to its friends.

The children returned from their trip inside. Though their hands couldn't be described as clean, they had made an effort to wash them. Sitting at the table, Beck eyed the tray of sandwiches, cookies, and grapes as if he hadn't had a bite to eat in weeks. Kate was sure it was all he could do not to grab a sandwich and gobble it down in one mouthful.

Kate suspected that Megan had told him to behave himself.

"Now can we eat?" Beck asked before Kate had a chance to sit down.

She laughed. "Go ahead. Help yourselves."

It had been a good many years since she'd had three children sitting around her table at mealtime. She recalled how Melissa, her middle child, had been the bossy one, telling Andrew and Rebecca how they should behave. But never before had any children been more appreciative of a sandwich and a few cookies than these three Maddock youngsters.

AFTER THE OLD TIMER'S DAY planning meeting, Paul and Sam Gorman went to the Country Diner for lunch. The diner was a popular gathering place for locals, especially at noon, but somehow they managed to snag the one remaining booth along the wall.

Paul slid across the blue-vinyl seat and plucked a menu from the holder.

"I think Loretta has meatball sandwiches as this week's special," Sam commented. "That's one of my favorites."

"Seems a little heavy for lunch." Paul quickly scanned down the menu. "Kate keeps reminding me to watch what I eat."

"That's the thing about wives, isn't it? They keep after you until you're eating healthy whether you like it or not."

Paul chuckled. "Probably means she wants me to stick around for a while."

Sam looked up when LuAnne, a longtime waitress at the diner, arrived with two glasses of water.

"Afternoon, Sam. Pastor Hanlon." LuAnne's hair was a shade of red that could only have come from a bottle, but it fit perfectly with her outgoing personality. "What'll you have this fine day?"

Paul closed his menu and pushed it aside. "I guess I'll try the tuna sandwich on rye and some of Loretta's fine coleslaw." The sweet-potato fries tempted him, but Paul knew Kate would disapprove.

"I'll go with the meatball sandwich and a slice of that cherry pie I saw." The fact that Sam was a bit overweight and had mild heart problems hadn't dampened his enjoyment of desserts a bit. "And coffee, if you will."

"Make that two coffees," Paul added, knowing full well that Loretta's coffee was strong enough to strip wallpaper.

LuAnne jotted down their orders on her pad. "You got it. I'll be back with your coffee in a sec."

While waiting for their coffee, Sam talked about his fishing exploits, promising to take Paul to a new fishing hole he'd recently discovered outside town.

LuAnne returned with two mugs of coffee and put them on the table along with a handful of tiny cream containers. "Loretta's a little behind on orders, but it shouldn't be too long."

"No hurry," Sam said.

Paul blew on his coffee to cool it. "So, how's business these days, Sam?"

"Same as usual, I guess. But somebody got into the Dumpster behind the Mercantile last night. Probably some kids got bored and decided to cause mischief. At my expense." He poured two creams into his coffee and added some sugar. "They dragged stuff out of the Dumpster and halfway down the alley. Took me an hour to clean up the mess first thing this morning."

The Mercantile that Sam owned was more than a grocery store. He carried almost anything folks might need, including camping supplies, knitting needles, and clothing for everyone in the family. He'd even special-order merchandise if he didn't carry what a person wanted.

"You have to wonder what gets into kids sometimes," Paul commented.

"I'd say lack of parental supervision is the problem."

Paul suspected that was at least part of the problem, and he counted his blessings that his own children had grown up with a minimal amount of fuss. He gave Kate most of the credit for that. And the Lord.

AFTER LUNCH, Paul called on a sick parishioner, then he dropped by the church to see if he had any messages and to work on his sermon for the next day. By the time he got home, it was almost dinnertime.

As he stepped into the living room, he glanced out the sliding-glass door to see how Kate's gardening project was coming along. Kate's helpers had apparently left for the day, but he smiled at the progress they'd made, noting the freshly installed plants along the back fence.

He found Kate working at the layout table in her studio, her tools and bits of stained glass all around her. It continually amazed him how she could transform sheets of colored glass into an intricate, artistic design. He certainly didn't have that kind of talent.

"The yard's looking good." He bent to kiss her hello.

She lifted her head to him and smiled. "It's a beginning."

"Were the kids all right? They seemed so eager, I didn't have the heart to send them away this morning. Did they run out of energy?"

"No, I did." She leaned back in her chair and brushed a wayward strand of hair back from her forehead. "I felt like I'd had enough for the day, and I knew the children were tired. Those youngsters should be playing, not working. I'm worried about them."

"Oh? In what way?"

"Their father is apparently in prison. I'm not entirely sure about their mother. The children tell me she's sick, but I think it may be more than that." Arranging three colored bits of glass in the form she'd laid out, Kate shook her head. "I feel like those children are being neglected, and they certainly act as though they're not being well fed."

"Do you want to alert the authorities?"

"I hate to do that unless I'm sure the children are at risk."

Paul could understand that. When a parent was reported for child neglect, it was hard to stop the bureaucratic machine once it got rolling. A false accusation could destroy a family.

"So what are you going to do?" he asked.

"After tomorrow's service, I think I'll take the family a casserole from the Faith Freezer . . . and a pie I'll make this evening. I'd like to talk to their mother. There's something strange going on with that family."

"A new mystery for you to investigate?"

"Could be."

"Do you know where they live?"

"I know the general area. Smoky Mountain Hollow. With any luck, I'll spot their mailbox or find someone to ask."

Paul suspected it might be harder to locate a specific family in the hollows than Kate anticipated, but he thought better of discouraging her. Once Kate decided that something needed investigating, there was no stopping her.

She looked at the sun catcher she was working on. Nodding to herself, she stood up. "How did your meeting go this morning?"

"Fine. The plans for Old Timer's Day are coming along nicely." Together they walked out of the room, which was actually a third bedroom Kate had converted into a studio to pursue her hobby. "Afterward, I had lunch with Sam. Apparently some vandals got into the Dumpster behind the store and made a mess last night. He wasn't too happy about that."

"I'm sure he wasn't."

"He did give me an idea for tomorrow's sermon, though."

"How we're supposed to clean up our messes?" Kate teased.

When they reached the kitchen, Paul stopped at the kitchen counter and leaned against it. Something cooking in the oven smelled delicious. He was hoping for pork-chop casserole and corn bread. After all, he'd restrained himself at lunch and skipped dessert.

"Not quite," he said. "Sam and I were talking about going fishing, so I thought I'd base my sermon on Genesis 1:28. God created man in his own image, then he admonished us to 'be fruitful and increase in number; fill the earth and subdue it. Rule over the fish of the sea and the birds of the air and over every living creature that moves on the ground.'"

"Which is the excuse you're going to use when you take a day off to go fishing with Sam?"

He gave her a look of mock innocence. "Of course not. I'm going to remind the congregation that not only does

humankind rule over God's creatures, but we have an obligation to protect them as well."

A grin spread across Kate's lips. "Which means you and
Sam are going fly-fishing and are going to catch and release
whatever hapless fish you manage to hook."

"Ah, you know me too well, Katie. Much too well." He
grinned at her, then went to wash up for dinner.

Chapter Four

As the church bell pealed to welcome parishioners to Sunday service, Kate took her place with the choir. Although she didn't view herself as having a particularly good voice, she usually managed to sing on key and did enjoy the camaraderie of the group. It was, she was sure, the only church choir that could claim a teacup Chihuahua as an unofficial member.

When Sam Gorman struck the first notes of the prelude on the organ, the congregation rose, and Paul walked to the plain wooden pulpit. He held his arms outstretched and welcomed the worshippers as he had so many times over the past thirty-some years, first in San Antonio and now in Copper Mill. Each time Kate saw him in his preacher's role, she was struck anew with his strong faith in the Lord.

The first hymn the congregation sang introduced Paul's theme for the day: *All things bright and beautiful, all creatures great and small, all things wise and wonderful, the Lord God made them all.*

Throughout the general announcements and offertory, Kate had trouble keeping her mind on the service. She kept thinking about the three Maddock children and wondering if they were all right. If they'd eaten a good breakfast and if their mother was taking care of them.

Are they in danger? Please, Lord, watch over and care for them.

She was so distracted that she missed the cue for the choir to stand for their final song, "Happy the Home When God Is There."

Livvy Jenner, who was sitting next to Kate, gave her a nudge with her elbow. Kate was so embarrassed by her lapse that she nearly dropped the choir book when she stood.

Fortunately, Livvy was unflappable, and she had the solo part. All Kate had to do was sing along in harmony, which she managed despite the heat of a blush that no doubt colored her cheeks.

When the service was over and the congregation had filed outside to visit in little groups, Livvy sought out Kate.

"Where were you this morning?" Livvy asked.

Livvy, a petite woman in her late forties, was Kate's best friend in Copper Mill and the head librarian in town. She wore her auburn hair in a short, casual style, and her hazel eyes shone with innate intelligence.

Kate frowned. "What do you mean where was I?"

"Well, you certainly weren't in church. It looked to me like you were ten thousand miles away, and wherever you were, you were worried."

"Oh dear, I didn't know it showed."

"So, what are you worried about?"

Kate slipped her arm through Livvy's and walked her away from the crowd to a shady spot near a flowering dogwood tree at the edge of the parking lot.

"Do you know the Maddock family? They live in Smoky Mountain Hollow. Three children. The oldest is named Megan, and she's in the seventh grade."

Slowly Livvy shook her head. "Not that I can recall. Most of the children around here have come to the library at one time or another, but I don't know all their names. Why do you ask?"

Briefly Kate told her how she'd met the children and about her concerns.

"There are a lot of families living in the hollows that really struggle to eke out a living. Jobs are pretty hard to find around here, particularly if you don't have a decent education or some skills."

Both Livvy and her husband, Danny, were native Tennesseans, had grown up in Copper Mill, and were now raising their two teenage boys here.

"Then paying a call on the family and taking some food wouldn't be out of line? I do want to make sure the children are all right."

"Some of the hill folks don't like charity. They've got too much pride. But it's still worth making the effort because of the children."

Kate was pleased that Livvy validated her instinct to check on the children's situation.

AFTER HER MIDDAY MEAL WITH PAUL, Kate packed up her Honda with a casserole and a cherry pie she'd baked. She took Smoky Mountain Road out of town. Soon, modern houses gave way to wooded areas. Small farm holdings and scattered homes were less well kept than those closer to town. To her dismay, she discovered the side roads weren't all marked, and many of the rural mailboxes displayed only house numbers, not family names.

At one point, a flock of wild turkeys—too skinny to grace a Thanksgiving table—strutted across the road, unconcerned by an approaching vehicle.

Finally she saw some children playing on a makeshift swing that hung from the branch of an ancient oak tree. She asked them where she could find the Maddock family.

When she pulled into the Maddocks' rutted driveway, she realized she'd driven more than two miles from town. She knew that a bus picked up the children for school every day in these outlying areas, but Megan and her siblings had obviously walked to Kate's house on Saturday and back home again. She'd had no idea how far they'd come to work in her garden with the hope of earning a little money.

They had precious little to hope for in their lives, she thought as she looked out her window at the run-down trailer. About forty feet long, it was propped up on cement blocks with weeds growing up around them. On a clothesline strung between two trees, children's shirts and jeans hung swinging in the breeze. An empty oil drum had been turned into a garbage can and was overflowing with trash, and a hodge-podge of power and phone lines crisscrossed between the trailer and a telephone pole.

Kate spotted Beck playing on the wooden porch that tilted at an angle in front of the door.

As she got out of the car, Beck hopped up and ran to the trailer's screen door, yanking it open. "Meg! Miz Hanlon's here!" he shouted.

Kate grimaced. If their mother was ill, that abrupt announcement wouldn't do much to improve Kate's welcome.

She had barely reached the steps to the porch with the casserole and pie in hand when Megan appeared along with Gwen. The clothes they wore were faded and showed a lot of hard wear. Neither girl was wearing a cap that afternoon, and their matching hair hung loosely past their shoulders.

Beck, she noticed, had been playing with several characters made out of cornhusks. Not traditional cornhusk dolls, but husks fashioned into a couple of cowboys and their horses. There was even a cornhusk corral and barn. Someone had used little scraps of fabric for the cowboys' hats and chaps. Very clever.

"Hey, Miz Hanlon," Megan said. The girls stepped out onto the porch, and Megan closed the screen door behind them. She looked at Kate with a hint of suspicion in her eyes. "Didn't expect you to come by."

"I thought since your mother hasn't been feeling well, she might enjoy not having to cook a meal. I brought you a casserole you only need to heat up and an extra cherry pie I thought you might like." She handed the pie to Beck.

"Wow!" He took the pie as though it were made of pure gold. "We never get to eat cherry pie."

Kate smiled at him. "Well, today you do. If it's all right with your mother," Kate added. "Is she in?"

"Ma's sleepin'," Megan said, almost too quickly.

"Yeah, sleepin'," Gwen confirmed.

Beck's gaze shot to his sisters, but he said nothing.

"Okay. I just wanted to meet her and tell her what a good job you three have been doing for me."

"I'll let Ma know you came by," Megan said.

"Yes, well . . ." At a loss for what she should do next, she focused on Beck's cornhusk cowboys. "I love your cornhusk dolls, Beck."

"They're not dolls. They're cowboys, like I'm gonna be when I grow up."

"I see. Well, they're very nice. Did someone make those for you?"

He looked up at his big sister. "She did."

"Really? You're very talented, Megan."

She shrugged. "I just do it when I get bored."

"She made me a whole family of dolls," Gwen volunteered. "Ma and Pa and three kids."

"That's impressive." She remembered Megan had also won a poster-drawing contest. She was an artistic young lady.

Kate felt foolish standing there with a casserole, talking about cornhusk dolls. Southern hospitality was generally more welcoming, but she decided to give the children and their ill mother a little slack.

She handed the dish to Megan. "Tell your mother to bake it at three hundred and fifty degrees for a half hour or so. You can bring the dish back to me when you come by next week."

"I'll tell her."

Gwen whispered something in Megan's ear.

The older girl frowned. "Sometimes our oven don't work too good. Can I cook this on top of the stove?"

"Yes." Kate hesitated. Once again, she had the feeling Megan was holding something back. A secret about her mother . . . or about the way the family lived?

"Put however much you want for your meal in a regular pan and warm it over a low heat. You'll have to stir it a couple of times so it won't burn."

"'Kay," Megan said. "Thanks."

Kate let a moment of silence go by, noticing that Beck had slipped his finger under the plastic wrap that covered the pie and dug out a cherry, which he'd popped into his mouth. From the red juice stuck to the corners of his lips, she suspected he'd sneaked more than one.

"Well, I'd better go. Tell your mother I hope she feels better soon."

"Sure," Megan responded noncommittally.

"Tell her to come visit when she can."

"I better go check on Ma now." Megan glanced over her shoulder past the screen door. "I hear her calling."

"Of course. You go ahead," Kate said.

Backing toward her car, Kate watched the three young faces stoically watching her. She turned to get into the Honda, and when she looked back at the porch, all she saw was the back of Beck as he followed his fleeing sisters into the trailer.

Kate would have bet anything that the children were going to heat up the casserole that minute and probably consume the entire pie before they ate the chicken and noodles. Almost assuredly, Beck would eat his share of pie right off.

Unless their mother intervened.

Kate had the distinct impression that wouldn't happen, and a shiver of unease traveled the length of her spine.

At least, though their mother was ill, she was apparently at home. Kate wondered why that thought didn't lessen her concern for the children.

THAT EVENING when Kate slid into bed beside Paul, she took his hand and squeezed it lightly.

"You're still worried about those kids, aren't you?" he asked.

"More than ever. I can't seem to get them out of my mind."

"Have you asked the Lord to help you out?"

"I have. Several times."

"Then he will. Be patient." Paul leaned over to kiss her good night.

Her husband was right, as usual. But patience wasn't one of Kate's strong suits. Particularly when she sensed something needed fixing.

Sighing, she lay on her back staring into the darkness. One of the big differences between San Antonio and Copper Mill was the absence of the light and noise Kate had grown accustomed to in the city. Gone were the streetlights, the sound of the neighbors coming and going, and the occasional flash of headlights past her windows. Whatever light that slipped in through the blinds at night came from the moon and stars. On moonless nights like this, with an overcast that hid the stars, the room was as dark as a West Virginia coal mine.

BY MORNING, Kate had come up with one way of finding out more about the Maddock family. After she'd spent extra time soaking up passages from Proverbs—specifically the ones about patience—Kate drove to the Copper Mill Elementary School. Arletta Walner, the school principal, would surely know the children and their mother.

Kate parked in a spot on the street in front of the kindergarten-through-eighth-grade school, which must have been in session because no students were loitering in the playground adjacent to the two-story brick-and-stucco building. An oversized cartoon of the school's mascot—a miner carrying a pickax and shovel—was painted on the school's wall that faced the playground. Below the painting was the school motto: We dig education.

A note on the front gate indicated that visitors should check in at the office.

Kate found Arletta behind the counter outside the principal's office talking with the school secretary. A buxom, gray-haired woman in her sixties, Arletta was the type of educator who could provide a soft shoulder for a student to cry on or be a stern disciplinarian, depending on the circumstances.

She looked up and smiled as Kate opened the door. "Be right with you."

"No rush."

Kate studied the notices on the counter—a PTSA meeting scheduled for the following week, a science fair happening in early May, and a lunch-hour band concert for Grandparents' Day. She smiled, remembering her stint on the PTSA board while her children were in school. How she had managed to fit in everything while working as an executive assistant in a San Antonio accounting firm was beyond her.

Arletta joined Kate at the counter. "Sorry to keep you waiting. The school superintendent is always after us for more paperwork, more forms. It's as if the administration doesn't think we have anything else to do—like teach the kids reading and 'rithmetic." She said the words with a smile, but Kate guessed they were also heartfelt.

"If you're busy—"

"No, no. I just like to complain. What can I do for you?"

Kate glanced around. "Could we talk in your office?"

"Of course." Immediately turning serious, the principal gestured for Kate to follow her.

Stacks of files were piled on the corners of Arletta's desk, and binders filled the bookcase below the window that looked out onto the playground. Kate sat in one of the two chairs in front of her desk.

"I hope you're not having a problem with one of our students," Arletta began.

"No, not at all. But I am concerned about the Maddock children." Kate explained how Megan had appeared in her yard looking for a job and her impression of the family.

Arletta listened carefully, all the time idly twisting a yellow pencil through her fingers.

"The Maddocks aren't well-off," she said when Kate finished talking. "But the children are well behaved. Megan's a sweet girl and very artistic."

"Yes, she told me she'd won an award."

Arletta nodded. "Gwen is a good student too. Becker's a bit of a problem, though. He's dyslexic, so reading is difficult for him. There's an aide in his class who helps out half days, but he really ought to be in a special program. I'm sure he gets frustrated and sometimes acts out. Maybe in a larger school system he'd do better." She shrugged. "But then, the larger school districts have their own problems."

"What do you know about their mother?"

The principal thought for a moment. "I met Glynis last fall at our open house. She seemed nice enough. Concerned about her kids, particularly Becker."

"What do you know about the children's father?"

"He wasn't at the open house that I know of. But I did see Glynis and a man in the Mercantile sometime before Christmas. I assumed he was the father."

Kate wasn't too sure how much she should reveal about the father's imprisonment. But Arletta seemed invested in the children as much or more than Kate was, so she decided it was worth the risk.

"Beck told me his father was in prison for killing someone."

That seemed to surprise Arletta. "Let me get their records." She left the room, and in a few minutes returned with several file folders.

Sitting back down at her desk, she flipped through the folders. "From these records, it looks like Glynis is a single mother and divorced. No father is listed, which usually means a custody dispute." She looked up from the file. "In this case, Mrs. Maddock might have been reluctant to name a man who's in prison for murder. The family moved to the district three years ago."

"Then the man you saw her with may have been a boyfriend," Kate thought out loud.

"Maybe. I don't keep track of the social lives of our parents."

Understandably, Kate thought. But the children hadn't mentioned anything about an adult male living with them. Or how long ago their father had been sent to prison. Perhaps Glynis was simply involved in a casual dating relationship. But what if it was something else entirely?

"Have you heard anything about Glynis being ill?" Kate asked.

"No, not at all. I could ask the children's teachers. They might know."

"I'm just concerned that the children are being neglected."

Arletta closed the files on her desk. "In this county, it's sometimes hard to know whether the problem is neglect or good old-fashioned poverty. My impression of Glynis Maddock was that she means well but lacks the resources she'd like to have."

"I can understand that." Kate wasn't totally satisfied. She suspected that something other than poverty might be going on in the Maddock household. Perhaps something related to Glynis' boyfriend, whom the children hadn't acknowledged?

She'd have to quiz Megan when she showed up that afternoon to help in the garden.

Chapter Five

Before going home, Kate stopped in at the Mercantile to pick up skim milk for Paul's morning cereal and some goat cheese that she liked to crumble in spinach salads along with dried cranberries and a low-fat berry dressing.

A bell tinkled above the door as she pushed her way inside the store. There was something very small-town and cozy about the Mercantile, with its narrow aisles and shelves stacked well above her head. Heaven help whoever was in the store if Tennessee had a major earthquake.

The refrigerated dairy section was at the back of the store. When Kate reached that aisle, she noted the storeroom door to the alley was standing open. Sam Gorman was taking one swipe after another with a big push broom and muttering to himself as he worked.

"If I ever catch the kids who are doing this, I'm going to personally tan their hides. Then I'll string 'em up by the thumbs, by golly!"

Raising her eyebrows, Kate couldn't recall seeing Sam this worked up before. It wasn't his usual style.

She peered out the back door. "What's wrong, Sam?"

He started, then leaned on his broom. "Sorry you overheard me ranting and raving. I'm just so tired of . . ." His voice trailed off as he looked up and down the alley on either side of the olive green trash bin. "This is the second time in less than a week that some kids have decided to ransack the Dumpster back here. They leave stuff strewn from here to the corner, and I've gotta clean up the mess."

"Paul mentioned you thought teenagers were rummaging in the Dumpster." Bits of paper had blown down the alley, and soggy cardboard looked as if it had been shredded. The bin itself was dented in places and had deep scratches on it, some of them fairly new. "How can you be sure they're teenagers?"

"Who else gets into this kind of mischief just for the fun of it? There's never anything worth having in there. It's mostly spoiled produce, lunch meat that's gone bad, and cereal packages that've been ripped open, plus empty crates and boxes I can't recycle."

"Maybe someone's looking for aluminum cans to recycle and make a little money."

"Well, they aren't going to find any cans in there. I keep those inside and turn 'em in myself when I get enough to make it worth the trip."

But a teenager who needed money might not know that. Or a youngster with hungry siblings. Someone desperate like Megan Maddock.

That tightened a thread of anxiety in Kate.

"Least they could do is clean up their own mess," Sam added.

"By any chance, do you know Glynis Maddock?" she asked.

He raked his fingers through his thick, brown hair. "Yeah, she shops here. I don't know her well, just to see her. She never talks much."

"When was the last time you saw her?"

He had to think for a moment. "I'm not sure. Of course, I'm not here every day, all day. She could've come in while I was off somewhere."

Off fishing if he had the chance, Kate suspected. "Have you seen her in the past couple of weeks?"

"Not that I can recall. She usually comes in around the first of the month to stock up, but it's been maybe six weeks or more since I've seen her." Using a dustpan, he scooped some debris he'd swept up and tossed it into the Dumpster. "Her older girl came in early last week looking for a job. Couldn't hire her, though. She's too young. Skinny little thing. She could sure use some meat on her bones."

"That's Megan. She's been helping me in my garden. I'm paying her a little bit. I think she's trying to help out her family."

"She seems like a good kid." He nodded as if to himself. "She came in Thursday or Friday last week and bought milk and bread, and a giant jar of peanut butter."

"The staff of life for some kids."

"For some grown men too." He gave her a wry smile. "The doc wants me to cut back on fatty foods like peanut butter. That's what I call a real sacrifice."

"It'll be worth it if you can stay healthy. And it doesn't do your heart any good to get so worked up over the mess someone made back here."

"Easier said than done, Kate. If these vandals hit me again, I'm gonna have to call in the sheriff."

She smiled, understanding his frustration. But maybe talking with her for a few minutes had helped reduce his anger.

On the other hand, the conversation had only managed to give Kate something more to worry about. Glynis Maddock hadn't been seen at the Mercantile for weeks, and her children were doing the shopping for her.

Could Megan be so desperate for money, or maybe food scraps, that she would Dumpster-dive to get a meal for herself and her siblings?

After Kate paid for the items she needed, she carried the groceries as far as her car, putting the bags in the trunk. Then she decided she'd take a minute to talk with Steve Smith at the gift shop on the southwest side of the Town Green. She wanted to ask about consigning a few stained-glass pieces for the Old Timer's Day craft booth.

Located in an old Victorian brick building, Smith Street Gifts had been founded by Steve's grandparents. Steve tried to feature local artists, and she was more than pleased to see a couple of her own stained-glass sun catchers featured in the shop's front window alongside Jessie Kilgore's lovely hand-made blue-and-white pottery.

When Kate entered the store, she found Steve restocking greeting cards in a round display boutique. Shelves along the wall and glass cases featured everything from quality jewelry to souvenirs for children stamped with the town's name on them.

"Hello, Kate." Steve set the remaining cards aside and

came toward the front of the store to greet her. "I'm glad you dropped by. I've been meaning to call you."

"Oh? What's up?"

"I've got a check for you. I've sold a couple of your hangings, and I'm hoping you can bring me some more of your work."

She felt a surge of pride. It was always a blessing to know that people had spent their hard-earned money to buy what she had created with her own two hands.

"I'm almost finished with a sunflower sun catcher." She'd sold a similar piece via her Web site recently and had decided to do a second one. "I can bring that in, maybe by the end of the week. And I've been toying with an idea for another lamp." Her gardening activities had been keeping her away from her stained-glass projects, but her creative mind was always buzzing with design ideas.

"Great. Let me get you that check."

She followed him toward his office in the back of the shop. A single man in his thirties, Steve had a quiet demeanor, and he was always neatly dressed in slacks and a white shirt with a tie when he was working at the store. She wondered that some local girl hadn't snapped him up yet. He'd make a good husband.

He handed her the check, and she grinned.

"I'm not quite ready to retire to the Caribbean, but it's a beginning." She tucked the check in her handbag. She'd use some of the money to buy more supplies for her studio, and the rest she'd donate to the Faith Freezer Program.

"I'm going to want some extra pieces for the craft booth at Old Timer's Day too."

"That's what I came in to ask you. Stained glass isn't exactly a traditional Appalachian craft."

He waved off her comment. "I've got a couple of ladies bringing quilts and an outfit that makes spin toys like old-fashioned yo-yos and dried-apple people. The more the merrier, I always say."

"Okay, I'll have to get busy then." Thinking about the additional supplies she'd have to order online, she started for the door, then stopped abruptly. "What about cornhusk dolls?"

"I didn't know you made those."

"I don't. But I know a young lady who's very talented artistically. She can do a lot with cornhusks, not only traditional dolls."

"Terrific. Tell her to drop by with some samples. If they're decent, they'll make a good addition for the booth at Old Timer's Day."

"She could sure use the money."

The corners of his hazel eyes crinkled with a smile. "I've never met an artist who couldn't use a few more dollars."

Shortly after three o'clock, Megan showed up in Kate's backyard with the empty casserole dish. Several strands of stringy blonde hair had come lose from her ponytail and trailed down past her shoulders.

"You finished the casserole already?" Kate removed her gardening gloves and took the dish that had been carefully washed.

"Beck ate the last of it this morning."

"For breakfast?"

The young girl shrugged. "He's like a garbage disposal. He'll eat anything."

And everything, Kate imagined. "That's what growing boys do." During his teen years, her son, Andrew, had been an eating machine.

"One time Beck ate a whole gallon of ice cream all on his own. Ma was really upset about that."

"Understandably. Did your mother enjoy the casserole?"

"Uh, yeah. Ma says thanks."

"I hope she's feeling better today."

"Same as always, I guess."

"What does the doctor say about her getting better?"

Shrugging, Megan's gaze darted toward the street as if she was about to bolt.

The girl's hesitancy, and Glynis' apparent invisibility of late, was becoming more and more troubling. Still, Kate didn't want to drive Megan away by asking too many questions.

Kate had half expected that Gwen and Beck would come with Megan today. Apparently they'd gone home on the school bus. To take care of their mother? Or were they on their own at home?

"I've started on the next flower bed, the little one on the east side of the house," Kate said. "More weeds, I'm afraid."

"That's okay. I don't mind pullin' 'em." Picking up a claw rake and weeding knife, the girl went right to work.

Kate knelt a few feet from Megan and resumed her weed pulling. "I thought I'd go to the nursery again tomorrow. I want to pick up some phlox and asters to put in the flower bed in the back and get some Texas bluebonnets for this sunny spot."

"Asters are pretty, but I've never seen any bluebonnets."

"They grow wild where I grew up in Texas."

Megan halted her attack on the weeds and sat back on her heels. "You came here from Texas?"

"I did. I was born and raised there."

The girl seemed to take a minute to process that news. "That's where the Alamo is, isn't it?"

"Indeed it is. Every youngster in Texas has to learn about the Alamo in their history classes."

"I bet Beck would like to go there sometime. He's crazy about cowboys 'n stuff."

"Well, maybe he will go to Texas someday. Where were you and your brother and sister born?"

Megan bent over her work again. "We came from Knoxville."

"Were your parents raised there?" Kate wondered if there were family members who could help out while the Maddocks were having hard times.

"I dunno." She resolutely averted her gaze.

This youngster was the most closed-mouthed girl Kate had ever met. Usually children would talk nonstop once they felt at ease with Kate. Megan didn't. She had secrets to keep, and Kate had the unsettling feeling that Megan had a good reason for keeping her own counsel.

They worked in silence for a while, with only a birdsong and the sound of an occasional passing car to interrupt the quiet afternoon.

"I stopped by Smith Street Gifts this morning," Kate finally said. "Have you been in there?"

"Sure. A few times. Just to look. I've never bought anything though."

"Steve Smith's the owner. He carries some of the stained-glass pieces I make on consignment."

Megan slanted a curious look in Kate's direction.

"It's just a hobby, really, but I enjoy making lamps and sun catchers," Kate admitted. "Steve's in charge of a craft booth for Old Timer's Day and is looking for craftspeople to feature their handiwork, for sale to the public. I was so impressed with the cornhusk dolls you made that I told him about you. He's interested in seeing some of your samples."

Megan's eyes rounded in astonishment. "He wants to *sell* my dolls? People would pay real money for them?"

"He'll have to take a look at them first. I don't know how much the retail price would be, but you'd probably get half of whatever he sells them for."

"I never thought about selling them. I just use old dried husks that everybody throws away."

"They're cleverly made, Megan. I love that you've created a whole matching family for Gwen, and that cowboy setup and barn for Beck is adorable."

"How much do you think they're worth?" She looked eager now, her expression filled with hope.

"I don't know. I don't have very good Internet access here at home, but you could use the library's computers to see what other people get for their dolls. I'm sure Steve would make you a fair deal."

"I've only used the school's computers, and we're not supposed to use them for personal stuff."

"I know what we can do," Kate said. "Instead of you coming here after school tomorrow, why don't we meet at the library. We'll look up cornhusk dolls and see what they're worth."

Megan appeared to weigh Kate's suggestion. "If it doesn't take too long, can I come back here to work some more?"

Clearly the girl was worried about the money she'd lose by not working.

"Of course you can. A Google search on the computer goes quite fast."

With a relieved smile, Megan went back to her task, tackling a two-foot-tall stalk of something with prickly leaves. She dug around the unwelcome guest in the flower bed, then yanked it out.

"Where do you usually get your cornhusks?" Kate asked.

"Mostly just when we eat corn in the summer. There's usually a vegetable stand out on the main road. Sometimes those folks will give me the husks they're throwing away or corn that's gone old on 'em. I've got a whole box full of husks."

Kate had an unwelcome thought. "I suppose Sam Gorman at the Mercantile tosses old ears of corn in the Dumpster behind his store."

"I don't know. I've never looked."

Kate hoped that Megan was telling the truth. Still, corn wasn't in season now. Megan and her siblings, driven by hunger, could have dug through the Dumpster more recently.

Kate didn't want to believe that.

When they'd cleared the weeds from the flower bed, Kate decided to call it a day.

"Would you like me to drive you home?"

Megan shook her head. "Naw, it's okay. I don't mind walking."

After a full day at school and two hours of gardening, Kate was sure Megan had to be tired. But once again, she didn't want to push the girl too hard.

"Okay, let me get some money for you." Kate went inside and returned with the money and a bag of apples. "Paul and I have a huge bag full of apples, and we won't be able to eat them all before they spoil. I thought maybe your family would enjoy them." Kate suspected that fruit and vegetables were low on the Maddock's priority list, well behind peanut butter.

"Sure. I guess." The girl took the money and shoved it in her pocket, then took the bag of apples. "Thanks."

"You're welcome. Tomorrow will be easier. No weeding, just planting."

Megan gave her a shy smile, then turned away to walk home by herself, leaving Kate to feel vaguely guilty that she hadn't insisted on driving her home.

What should I do about that girl, Lord?

WHEN PAUL CAME HOME, Kate was in her studio sorting through bits and pieces of cobalt blue glass for the background of her sunflower sun catcher.

"I'm in here," she called to him.

She sensed him enter the room but didn't look up. "How was your day, dear?"

"Typical Monday. One parishioner called to say my sermon yesterday wasn't up to its usual standard. Another called to let me know it was the best sermon she'd ever heard."

"Oh dear." Smiling, Kate looked up from her glass sorting. "If it means anything, I side with whoever said your sermon was great."

"You're the most important member of the congregation as far as I'm concerned. And the tie breaker." He crossed the room to give her a kiss. "Thank you for your vote of confidence."

"Anytime."

"Were you in town today?"

"I was. Among other things, I stopped by to see Steve Smith. He'd sold a couple of my stained-glass pieces and wants more for the store and for Old Timer's Day."

"I thought he would. Did you hear what happened at Emma's Ice Cream Shop?"

"No. What?"

"Someone broke in through the back door last night. Got into the ice-cream freezer and made off with two of those big five-gallon containers of ice cream. Emma found them a block down the street this morning. Ripped apart at the seams and empty."

Kate's first thought was that Beck had consumed more than one gallon of ice cream. But that didn't seem possible. Or reasonable. He was only nine years old. No youngster that age could eat that much ice cream without exploding. He'd certainly have trouble ripping the heavy cardboard apart without the help of someone bigger and stronger as well.

"Sam's Dumpster was ransacked again last night too," she told Paul. "He was really upset."

"Sorry to hear that." Paul picked up a six-inch square of onyx red glass and held it up to the overhead light to look through it. "Skip Spencer came over to Emma's to take a look at the crime scene, but I'm not sure how easy this case will be for our young deputy to solve."

"He's a sweet young man and an eager police officer, but he's got a lot of growing to do," Kate agreed.

In terms of being an amateur social worker, Kate knew she had a lot of growing to do too. Then again, she had no right to interfere in a family's life if the mother was present in the household, even if things weren't as Kate would have liked them to be. She couldn't run roughshod over Glynis Maddock.

But that would change if she didn't get a clearer picture of the children's situation and what danger they might be in soon.

Chapter Six

Early the next morning, Kate made another trip to Jenkins Nursery, this time to pick up flats of bedding plants—blue phlox and asters and mixed petunias. She had to special-order a flat of bluebonnets. Floyd Jenkins told her they'd arrive in a few days.

In some ways, designing a garden was like designing one of her stained-glass pieces. Colors complemented each other, and the eye saw the whole in a different way than it would when viewing a single piece of glass or an isolated flower.

An overcast sky threatened rain, and Kate barely made it home in time to set out the flats of flowers she'd purchased, change clothes, and toss together a green salad for the potluck luncheon that followed the women's Bible study at church.

Slightly breathless as she descended the stairs to the all-purpose room in the church basement, Kate found Millie Lovelace and Dot Bagley already there.

"I do hope we'll be able to start this meeting on time. I have to get to the SuperMart right after lunch," said Millie, the sixty-year-old part-time church secretary.

"You can always leave early." Dot had spread a white table-cloth over a long folding table and was putting out paper napkins and silverware for the luncheon. "Of course, we'd miss you," she quickly added with a sweet smile.

Kate placed her salad bowl on the table beside the plate of deviled eggs Dot had brought.

"I do have one item I'd like the group to discuss before we all have to leave," Kate said.

"If it's not on the agenda, we won't have time." Millie straightened the napkins Dot had placed on the table.

"It will take only a minute or two." Kate realized she shouldn't have brought up the issue with time-conscious Millie. "It's something Paul wants me to ask the ladies."

"Oh." That seemed to give Millie pause. Paul was her boss, after all, though you wouldn't know it by the way Millie ran the church office.

Others began arriving, including Phoebe West, who carried her sleeping infant in a cuddly sling across her chest. Patricia Harris, always trim and neat with her short blonde hair, fol-lowed right behind Phoebe.

As soon as most of the women were present, they sat down in a circle of folding chairs. Dot Bagley opened the meeting with a short prayer, then everyone got out their Bible-study material.

"Before we get into today's lesson, I have something I'd like to discuss," Kate said. Before Millie could object, she added, "It won't take long."

Seeing nods of agreement from everyone except Millie, Kate launched into the plans for Old Timer's Day and the food booth she hoped the ladies would support with their time and their baked goods to raise money for the Faith Freezer Program.

Martha Sinclair, a steady volunteer since the beginning of the Faith Freezer Program, spoke up first. "I think that's a wonderful idea. We need the money to buy staples, and I'd like more people to learn about the service in case they know of someone who could use our help. I'll bring two cakes to sell. What about the rest of you?"

Her enthusiastic support seemed to spur the women into action. They volunteered to work in shifts to cover the hours the event took place and agreed to donate cakes and pastries.

Millie glanced at her watch, and Kate decided to get the lesson going. She nodded to Patricia Harris, who began the lesson about Jesus feeding the multitudes with a few scant fish and loaves of bread.

A lesson those who so willingly gave of themselves to support Faith Freezer had already learned, Kate realized. *Thank you, Lord.*

BY THE TIME KATE WENT HOME then started for town to meet Megan at the library, the rain had begun in earnest. She wished now that she'd suggested picking Megan up at the school so she wouldn't have to walk in the rain. Hopefully Megan had thought to wear a rain jacket when she left home that morning.

Kate hurried up the steps of the two-story brick building. Once under the eaves, she shook the rain from her umbrella, folded it up, and pulled open the impressive oak door. Inside, the air felt warm, and there was the faint scent of old paper and ink, contrasting with the sight of modern electronic catalog terminals near the horseshoe-shaped front counter.

Livvy was working behind the counter, her reading glasses perched on top of her head.

"Hey, Kate," the head librarian said in greeting. "What brings you out on such a wet day?"

"I'm meeting Megan Maddock here after school. She's the girl I told you about."

"The family that lives out in Smoky Mountain Hollow?"

"Right. Megan makes very creative cornhusk dolls, and Steve Smith thinks he might want to take some on consignment for an Old Timer's Day craft booth. We're going to check the Internet to see what similar dolls are selling for."

A twinkle brightened Livvy's hazel eyes. "I see your hand at work here. You think that could be a way for the girl to make a little extra money to help her family."

"She is very talented."

The door to the library burst open, admitting a chilly gust of wind along with three young adolescent boys. Laughing and dripping rainwater on the carpet, they bumped against each other in good fun.

"Easy, guys," Livvy admonished them. "Library rules."

The youngsters grimaced but quieted down, making their way to a table at the back of the fiction section.

"Sometimes on rainy days the kids like to come here instead of hanging out at the school yard or going home," Livvy commented without rancor. "Fortunately, I love 'em all. Well, most anyway."

Kate could understand Livvy's ambivalence about the somewhat noisy invasion of her domain.

When the library door opened again, it was Megan. Drenched to the skin, her stringy long hair was dark blonde and dripping from the ends. Her old T-shirt clung to her narrow frame, and her sneakers left a trail of damp footprints across the carpet.

"Oh, Megan, you're soaked. I should've picked you up at school." Kate hurried to the girl. "Let's get you to the restroom. At least we can dry your hair with some paper towels."

Megan tried to wring out her wet hair. "I'm okay, ma'am."

"I guess you didn't think it was going to rain today and forgot your jacket."

"Yes, ma'am. I forgot . . . ," she mumbled. She glanced quickly toward the back of the library where the older students had commandeered a study table, then just as quickly looked away.

Kate heard one of the three boys in the back say something she couldn't quite make out, but she knew the remark was aimed at Megan and wasn't complimentary. The other boys laughed.

"Where are the computers?" Megan kept her head down.

Kate's heart ached for the girl. It was no fun to be singled out as the butt of some boy's joke, particularly for an adolescent struggling to find her way to womanhood. "They're upstairs. Let's go."

Holding her head high and fixing her eyes on the boys to let them know she'd heard the remark, Kate led Megan up the stairs.

This area was quieter than the first floor and housed the nonfiction section, meeting rooms, and a bank of computers for public use.

"Why don't you pick a computer, and I'll show you how to Google for what you want to find," Kate suggested.

"Oh, I know Google, ma'am. We use that at school."

Kate chuckled at herself. "Guess I lost track of what you kids are learning these days."

Megan pulled a chair up to the first computer and sat down. Within moments, she'd connected to the Internet, brought up the Google search engine, and typed in "cornhusk dolls" in the window.

Almost instantly, the screen filled with related Web sites, most of them about how to make cornhusk dolls.

"Since you already know how to make the dolls, let's narrow our search by adding the word *buy* to the key terms," Kate suggested.

Again, dozens of links appeared. Megan began working her way through them one at a time. She clicked through pictures of dolls and checked the prices.

"Look at that!" Megan exclaimed as she came across the most expensive doll she'd found. "They want sixty bucks for that old-fashioned doll. I could make it for nothin'. Cornhusks don't cost a penny." She leaned closer to the screen. "That fancy-dancy hat she's wearing wouldn't be hard to make either. Just a little swatch of material. The apron too."

Megan spent another half hour going through Web sites before she turned to Kate. "Is Mr. Smith really going to pay me something for the dolls he sells?"

"You bet."

"Wow! If he only paid me half"—she did the mental calculation—"that could be as much as thirty dollars for just one doll."

"Well, that would have to be a very elaborate doll. Yours are a little simpler in style, but they're still worth good money. At least, I think so."

"Wow," Megan said again before moving her chair away from the computer. "I'd better get busy makin' a bunch of dolls for Old Timer's Day."

Based on that comment, Kate suspected she'd lost her gardening helper. "I thought you'd want to. You need to talk to Steve Smith too. He'll be able to help you figure out the kinds of dolls that are likely to sell best."

Her eyes alight with enthusiasm, Megan walked downstairs beside Kate. "I can drop by the gift shop after school one day this week," Megan said.

Looking out the window, Kate could see that a late-afternoon gloom had settled in, and it was still raining. *No gardening today*, she thought.

Kate waved good-bye to Livvy and said to Megan, "My car's right down the street. I'll drive you home."

"You don't have to do that. I can walk."

"I can't let you do that. Your hair and clothes are just barely starting to dry. I know the school bus has already gone. You'll catch your death if you walk all the way home in this downpour."

"I've walked in the rain before," Megan said stubbornly.

Kate wrapped her arm around the girl's shoulders. "If I let

you walk home and you catch a cold, I'll feel terribly guilty. I'll probably lay awake all night praying and worrying about you," she explained. "So letting me drive you home would be a favor to *me*, okay?"

Megan eyed her suspiciously, and then a little smile tugged at her lips. "A favor, huh?"

"Yes." Kate laughed. "Come on."

Stepping out the door, she opened her umbrella. Side by side, the two made a dash for the Honda, their feet splashing in puddles that had formed on the pavement. Rain drummed on the umbrella like an acoustic band. Wind gusted, sending tree branches into a gyrating dance.

They reached the car and separated, Kate sliding behind the steering wheel while Megan climbed in the passenger side.

"Whew! That's some spring shower." Kate put the closed umbrella on the floor of the backseat. "I'll get the heater going in a second. That'll warm you up."

The girl wrapped her arms around herself. "I'm okay."

Except for the goose bumps Kate could see on Megan's bare arms, she might have believed the girl. The child tried so hard to be independent, so grown-up.

Few cars were on the street as Kate pulled away from the curb, and the streetlights had automatically turned on, though they did little to cut through the gloom. The windshield wipers worked frantically to clear away the rain.

"Would you have really prayed for me?" Megan asked.

Kate glanced at Megan. "Of course I would. In fact, I've already prayed for you." *A good many times*.

"Why?"

Kate smiled as she turned onto the road to Smoky

Mountain Hollow. "Well, because I like you, and I want God to watch over you and your brother and sister. Your mother too."

"I don't think anybody's ever prayed for me before."

A sharp ache filled Kate's chest. "I'm sure they have, Megan. I have a whole list of people I pray for every day, even if I don't tell them about it all the time. My children, of course. They're all grown-up, but I still pray for them. And my grandchildren, and my husband. I also pray for people in the church who are sick or facing troubles."

"Do you ever pray for yourself?"

"Oh yes. Every day. But I try not to pray for material things. Mostly I ask for God's guidance and his help to achieve his plan for me."

"Does he listen?"

"I believe he does, yes."

Megan grew quiet and thoughtful, and Kate hoped she had touched the girl's heart in some small way that would help her reach out to the Lord.

The windshield wipers continued their steady beat as rain washed over the car.

As they turned onto the gravel drive leading to the Maddocks' trailer, Megan said, "Do you think God would listen to me?"

"I'm sure he would. You just have to open your heart to him." Kate brought the car to a halt in front of the trailer.

Megan stared straight ahead at her run-down home with its tilted porch and the rain-soaked laundry hanging on the clothesline. "What do I say?"

"To God?" Kate felt the girl's struggle, her fears and hopes, the pain of growing up in a difficult situation. "All you have to do is talk to him." She touched her own chest. "Right from your heart. He'll understand you."

Slowly Megan reached for the door handle.

"How about I come in and meet your mother?" Kate spoke hastily, not wanting to lose contact with Megan. "You're late getting home, and she might be worried about you."

She shook her head. "Ma's not home."

"Oh? She went out somewhere?" As Kate thought about it, she'd never seen a car parked by the trailer. Where would Glynis have gone without a vehicle, in the rain?

"She's away. That's all."

Reaching for the girl's arm, Kate stopped Megan before she could get out. "What do you mean, she's away?"

"Just gone. It's no big deal."

"Megan, it's time for you to be honest with me. How long has your mother been gone?"

"She went away for the weekend. She'll be back. I gotta go—"

"How long ago did she leave?"

Angry, Megan turned on her. "It's none of your business, okay? And don't go calling children's services or anything dumb like that. We're getting along fine. Stay out of it and leave us alone." Tears filled her eyes and threatened to spill over.

"Megan, I'm making it my business because I care about you," she said softly. "I know you're in trouble and are afraid of something. I've sensed it all along. Now tell me what's going on."

The girl's chin trembled. "She told me not to tell anyone."

"Don't you think it's a secret you've kept long enough?"

Swiping at her eyes with the heels of her palms, Megan tried to stanch the flow of tears. "Ma left about six weeks ago. She made sure we had plenty of food in the house, and she left me with some extra money. She was gonna come right back after the weekend. She promised. But she hasn't, and I don't know what to do. I'm so . . . s-s-scared."

Chapter Seven

Kate took Megan in her arms as she would her own child and held the girl tight. The danger, it seemed, was even more serious than Kate had realized.

"It'll be all right, honey," she soothed, fighting the threat of her own tears.

At thirteen, Megan shouldn't have been faced with such an adult responsibility, having to hold her family together and care for her younger siblings. It was too big a burden for her slender shoulders to bear.

"Shh, now, we'll work it out. I promise."

"But why hasn't Ma come home?" Megan sobbed and hiccuped.

"I don't know, honey." But sure as the sun rose in the East, Kate was going to find out. Rich or poor, what mother would desert her children for six weeks? It was beyond comprehension. "Has your mother called you?"

Sniffling, Megan shook her head. "The phone company turned off the phone. I think Ma forgot to pay the bill."

Kate found a tissue in her purse and handed it to Megan.

"Let's get you inside. You can change out of your wet clothes, and we'll talk about—"

"You can't tell *anyone* that Ma's gone, Miz Hanlon. You can't!" She wiped her eyes and blew her nose.

"But you need help," Kate said.

"If you tell, children's services will come after us kids. They'll separate us and put us in foster care. Ma will never be able to find us again, and I won't be able to take care of Gwen and Beck."

It sounded as if Megan had either been told dire tales about the foster-care system or been a part of it at one time.

"What makes you think you'd be separated? I understood they tried to keep siblings together."

"But they can't. Practically nobody wants three kids. And Beck's dyslexic. Sometimes he gets really frustrated and angry. They'd stick him someplace just to get rid of him. Gwen would be okay, if she's lucky."

"And you?"

"I'm a teenager." She said the word as though announcing she was a rattlesnake. "They'd put me in some stupid group home with a bunch of druggies and dropouts."

Gently, with her heart nearly breaking for the child, Kate pushed Megan's straight hair back from her face. "How do you know all this?"

She shrugged. "Other kids. Ones at school. And where we used to live." She swallowed hard. "Ma told me to take care of Gwen and Beck. I can't break my word. I'll take them and run away if I have to, but we're not going to foster care." She set her chin at a determined angle that said she meant business.

"At this point, no one is threatening you with foster care.

I'm just trying to help you." *Please, Lord, I need your help more now than ever. What should I do?*

"Beck said your father's in jail?"

Megan nodded.

"Do you have any aunts or uncles who could look out for you until your mother comes back?" *If she's coming back,* Kate thought with a combined surge of anger and fear for the children.

"Nope."

"Grandparents?"

The teen shook her head.

"Close friends of the family? Maybe one of your neighbors here?" There had to be someone who could love and care for these children.

"There's nobody. Ma doesn't like any of these neighbors and doesn't talk to 'em. Says we're supposed to stay clear of 'em. I'm the only one that can take care of Gwen and Beck."

But you're only thirteen, Kate wanted to say. Not that it would have made any difference to Megan. Not when she'd made up her mind that there were no other choices available. As an adult, Kate knew there had to be.

The most obvious choice was for the children to move in with her and Paul, temporarily.

"Let's go inside. The three of you can pack up a few things. You're coming to my house."

Megan stared at her blankly. "We're okay like we are."

"How much food do you have in the house? Have you got anything besides peanut butter to eat? Gwen and Beck are too little to go without healthy meals." She softened her tone.

"You're not okay, honey. No one should have expected you to be okay for this long. You can stay with me and my husband. Together we'll figure out what to do."

Megan's chin started to tremble again, and she bit her lip. "What if Ma comes back? She won't know where we've gone."

"We'll leave her a note."

"You're not going to call children's services, are you?"

"No, I won't call anyone, unless I absolutely have to, and that's certainly not going to happen tonight."

Kate went into the trailer with Megan. The living room-kitchen combination was neater than she might have expected. Beck and Gwen were sitting on a tired salmon-colored couch watching a static TV. They looked up in alarm.

"It's all right," Kate said. "I know your mother's away, so you three are going to come spend a few days with me."

They checked with Megan to be sure she approved of the plan.

Since they didn't have suitcases, Kate found some large black garbage sacks for them to fill with their clothes and personal items. While they were packing, she walked over to the phone on the kitchen counter, planning to leave a note for Glynis.

She moved aside a pile of school papers, searching for something to write on. Beneath the clutter, what she found made her blood run cold.

On a notepad, someone had printed the words *Run! Run!! Run!!!* in increasingly large letters as though they were terrified. The handwriting looked decidedly adult.

Was Glynis in trouble? Is that why she hadn't returned?

Had she been warned of the danger and fled? *Without her children?*

Tearing off the note, she slipped it into her handbag. Then she wrote her own message, leaving her name and phone number so Glynis could reach her and the children. *If* she returned.

On a hunch, she picked up the phone. No dial tone.

The unpaid telephone bill was stuck under the phone. Kate took a quick look. She wrote down Glynis' phone number listed on the bill and dropped that in her purse as well.

Megan appeared from the back of the trailer carrying a heavy black garbage bag over her shoulder and shoving a cardboard box in front of her with her feet.

Puzzled, Kate asked, "What's in the box?"

"My cornhusks and some ol' scraps of material. If I'm going to make more dolls, I've gotta have my stuff."

"Of course."

"Beck's good jeans are out on the clothesline. I gotta go get 'em and the other stuff too." Megan headed for the door.

"No, you've gotten soaked enough for one day." Kate pulled the last empty garbage bag from the box. "You make sure Gwen and Beck have everything they need and use the umbrella to walk them to the car. I'll be right there. And lock the front door on your way out."

"The lock's broken. Has been forever. We don't have anything worth stealing anyway. The TV barely even works."

From the looks of things, Kate figured that was probably true.

As she hurried out the door and around to the side of the

trailer where the laundry was hanging, she noticed that some-one had tipped over the trash can and strewn the contents across the yard. She wouldn't take time to pick up the soggy mess now.

Even though the rain had slowed, Kate worked quickly, snatching the sopping wet clothes from the clothesline and dropping them in the bag. She'd run them through the dryer at home.

She was reaching for the last piece, one of Beck's T-shirts, when she heard a rustling noise in the nearby stand of trees.

Thinking one of the children had come out to retrieve something, she turned. "We can come back tomorrow—"

No one was there. Only shadowed woods.

A tremor of fear prickled the hairs on the back of her neck.

She dropped Beck's T-shirt into the bag.

When she looked up, she saw something moving between the trees and quickly vanish into the dark shadows.

A person? An animal? The culprit who'd turned over the trash can?

Run!

Hastily she picked up the bag and hurried to the car.

PAUL'S PICKUP WAS IN THE GARAGE when Kate arrived home with the children. She parked the Honda beside the truck.

Paul opened the door that led from the house to the garage, calling to Kate. "Hi, honey, I was beginning to—"

Megan got out of the car, quickly followed by Gwen and Beck. Kate popped the trunk before she exited the car.

"Paul, you remember the Maddock children—Megan, Gwen, and Beck. They're going to be staying with us for a while."

Visibly surprised, he quickly recovered. "Terrific. We always like having company. Come on in." He held the door open.

"Come on, kids. Grab your things from the trunk. Megan, you can put your box of supplies in my studio under the drawing table."

Megan made sure her siblings got their own bags and carried them inside. She trudged in after them.

"Could you get the air mattress out?" Kate asked Paul. "I'll have to put the girls on the foldout couch in your study. We can use that portable privacy screen that's in the garage and make a space for Beck in the corner of the living room. He can sleep on the air mattress."

"What's going on?" Paul whispered.

"Their mother left six weeks ago and hasn't been heard from since," she whispered back, reaching up to kiss him.

He touched her damp hair. "Looks like you got caught in the rain."

"I did. We'll talk more later."

All three children were huddled together in the middle of the living room. Although they'd been inside the house once before to use the restroom, they looked lost.

"This is the biggest living room I've ever seen," Beck said.

"This house belongs to the church. It's the parsonage," she explained. "Sometimes we have church meetings here, which is why this room is so large."

"We've never lived in a house with a fireplace." Gwen

cautiously approached the river-rock fireplace in the corner and peered up at the chimney.

Paul appeared from the garage with the air mattress.

"Maybe after dinner Paul can start a fire for us," Kate said. "Right now we'd better get the beds made up. Paul, can you and Beck blow up the air mattress? You know where the extra sheets and blankets are. The girls and I will handle the foldout couch."

"Got it." Paul hooked one arm around Beck's shoulders. "Come on, buddy. Let's get you set up for where you're going to sleep."

After the beds were made up, Kate started dinner. Spaghetti seemed like the easiest thing to pull together in a hurry. Besides, it was a dish universally enjoyed by youngsters.

She put a pound of ground meat in a frying pan to brown for the sauce and got down one of her largest pots to cook the pasta.

"Do you children have homework?" she asked as they wandered into the kitchen.

"Do we gotta do homework?" Beck complained.

"You bet you do. When my children were growing up, they did their homework right on that oak table over there. Go get whatever you need. Paul will help you."

Beck remained reluctant but did as he was told. Megan said she'd done her homework during a free period at school and sat down to help Gwen with her math.

Kate was struck by how familiar the scene appeared. Three youngsters at her old oak table, well-chewed pencils in hand, laboriously doing their schoolwork. Paul had the patience of Job as he worked with the boy, even when Beck lost control and threw his pencil across the room.

"I can't do this!" Beck screamed. He folded his arms across his narrow chest and stubbornly pushed out his lower lip.

Megan and Gwen watched expectantly for what would happen next.

Paul gave Beck a moment to pout before he interceded. "You know what, buddy? There are lots of things I can't do. But if it's something important, like schoolwork, then God wants me to at least try."

"God doesn't care about any ol' schoolwork."

"He cares about you. That's the important thing. He doesn't need you to be perfect in everything you do, but he does want you to do the very best you can."

Beck laid his head down on his arm. "I'm stupid."

"I don't think so," Paul said. "God made some people good at math and some good at spelling and some good at sports. What are you good at, Beck?"

"Nothin'."

"He's a real good artist," Megan volunteered. "He likes to paint and color and things like that."

"Me too," Gwen said. "I like to draw houses and people and trees and dogs. We've never had a dog, but I want one someday."

"Really?" Paul leaned back in his chair and winked across the room at Kate. "How about flying kites? Have you ever done that?"

Suddenly interested, Beck lifted his head. "Nuh-uh."

"Well, now, let me tell you about the kite contest we're going to have right here in Copper Mill."

Listening to her husband explain the Old Timer's Day kite decorating and flying contest, Kate got down a jar of homemade spaghetti sauce she'd made with tomatoes she'd bought from a local farmer. She poured the sauce into one of her Mauviel pans and added the browned meat.

By the time the sauce was simmering, the noodles had cooked, a tossed green salad had been made, and Beck had struggled through the rest of his homework—motivated by Paul's promise to help all the children make kites.

"Time to set the table," Kate announced. "Gwen, you can do the silverware. And Megan, would you get some plates down for us, please?" Kate gestured toward the cupboard that contained the dishes. "Beck, how about clearing off the table for us?"

The children scurried around to do their respective tasks. Soon everything was ready, and they all sat down at the table. Beck's eyes were so wide, he looked as though he was ready to jump into the big bowl of spaghetti and eat it all by himself.

"One of our customs is to say grace before dinner. Will you join us?" Kate asked.

Hesitantly, as though unfamiliar with the tradition, the children folded their hands in front of them. Kate nodded for Paul to begin.

"Dear Lord, thank you for bringing Megan, Gwen, and Beck to stay with us for a while. Help us to be kind to each other and learn your loving ways. Bless this food to your service and guide us along your path. Amen."

Kate echoed her husband's "Amen."

"Can I ask God to bring back our Ma?" Megan asked.

"Of course," Paul said.

Megan squeezed her eyes tightly shut. "God, I don't know if you can hear me or not. But if you can, would you please find our Ma and bring her back home? We miss her something fierce. Amen."

Kate pressed her lips together, struggling against the burn of tears in her eyes. *Please, Lord, hear Megan's prayer and help these children.*

AFTER DINNER, the children helped clear the table. Kate washed the dishes, and Megan dried them while the other two youngsters took their baths. Meanwhile, Paul laid a fire in the fireplace.

Later they all sat around enjoying the fire, but it didn't take long before the younger children's eyelids began to droop. Kate hustled them off to bed and tucked them in with a kiss.

When she returned to the living room, she sat down in her favorite rocker. Paul was in his chair reading a biography of a famous church leader. Megan was sitting cross-legged on the floor, mesmerized by the fire.

"Megan, where did your mother say she was going?" Kate asked softly so she wouldn't disturb Beck, who was sleeping on the cot in the far corner of the room.

Megan glanced in Kate's direction. "Nashville. She likes country music."

"Did she go alone or with a friend?"

The girl lowered her gaze and spoke softly. "A friend."

Kate had an inkling of who that friend might be. "A boyfriend?"

Megan nodded.

So Glynis Maddock had left her children to go off with her boyfriend six weeks ago, apparently telling Megan she'd only be gone for the weekend. Kate tried very hard not to judge the woman, but Glynis' actions suggested she wouldn't be nominated for a Mother of the Year award anytime soon. "Do you know the man's name?"

Megan sighed. "Hank Weller. He's not very nice, but Ma likes him, I guess."

Sometimes lonely women made bad decisions about men. It sounded to Kate as if Glynis might have fallen into that trap.

Or had she left because someone had told her to run?

Chapter Eight

By the time Kate slid into bed beside her husband, she was bone weary in the same way she'd grown tired after a day with her own young children.

She took Paul's hand. "You were wonderful helping Beck with his homework. Very patient."

"He'll be fine if the adults around him are encouraging. I had a friend in elementary school who was dyslexic. Everybody called him dumb or stupid."

"But you didn't." She smiled into the darkness, confident her husband had never been cruel to anyone.

"No way. He might have had trouble with reading, but he was a whiz on the soccer field. I always wanted to be on his team. He also worked harder on academics than any kid in our class, and he overcame a lot. Last I heard, he was a judge in Nashville."

She squeezed his hand. "Good for him. And you."

"I'm worried about you and the Maddock family, honey. I love that you care about the kids, but I hope you're not getting in too deep. We don't know anything about the children's mother or why she left."

"I know, but that's what I'm going to find out." Kate was silent for a moment, pondering her fear that both Glynis and the children were in danger. "At least they'll be safe here with us until I can figure out what's going on."

Paul leaned over to kiss her. The last thing she heard before falling asleep was his whispered "I love you, Katie."

THE NEXT MORNING, Kate rose extra early to pack lunches for the children and fix them oatmeal for breakfast. For however long they stayed with her, she was determined to see that they were well fed.

As Kate prepared the oatmeal—which she gussied up with strawberries, brown sugar, and a few chocolate chips—she thought about what a task it was to take care of three children. Besides being well fed, they also needed to be well clothed.

She turned to the kids, who were now all seated at the oak table waiting for breakfast. Beck's jeans were three inches too short, Gwen's little shirt had a button missing, and Megan wore a baggy flannel shirt that probably belonged to her mother. No wonder the boys teased her.

All the children needed new clothes. And haircuts. In fact, an entire makeover would be the perfect treat for Gwen and Megan, Kate decided as she finished garnishing the final bowl of oatmeal.

She'd talk to Betty Anderson, the proprietor of Betty's Beauty Parlor. Betty and the beauticians working for her might be willing to make over the Maddock children as a philanthropic project. It wouldn't be the first time that Betty, who had such a generous spirit, had performed an act of kindness for someone in the community.

But first things first. She needed to track down Glynis Maddock. Fortunately, the storm had passed during the night, leaving a bright blue sky and cool temperatures.

She drove the children to school, saw them safely onto the grounds, and was waiting at the library when Livvy unlocked the door.

"Goodness, did you forget something yesterday?" With a teasing glint in her eye, Livvy held open the door for Kate.

"Not really. I just have a research project I'm anxious to start."

Livvy switched on the lights and went behind the counter. "What are you researching this time?"

"I'm trying to find a missing person."

Livvy reacted with surprise. "Shouldn't you be talking to Sheriff Roberts?"

"I don't want to involve the authorities unless I have to." Kate had made a promise to Megan, and she was determined to keep that promise as long as she could. "I thought I'd start with Google and see where that leads me."

Upstairs, Kate sat down in front of the same computer she and Megan had used the previous afternoon and brought up Google again. When she typed in "Glynis Maddock," all she got were references to a woman in England. Definitely not the missing mother she was seeking.

She tried the white pages for past addresses in Knoxville and a people-search function that turned up nothing useful. Basically, Google had never heard of Glynis.

"Think this through, Kate," she said out loud. "Glynis was going to Nashville. How do you find her?"

She brought up lists of motels. There were hundreds. Even if she called them all, Glynis might not be registered under her own name. Hank Weller could have signed a registration form. Or they could be staying with friends, which would make the search impossible.

Then a thought struck Kate. Maybe Glynis hadn't come home because she'd been hurt.

From a quick search, she learned that there were ten hospitals in Nashville. Kate wrote down the phone numbers, but she wasn't optimistic.

She tried Googling Hank Weller but had no better luck than she'd had with her search for Glynis.

Out of ideas, Kate leaned back and stared at the computer screen. "Where are you, Glynis? Your children need you."

The troubling thought that Glynis had run away from some danger nagged at the back of Kate's mind. How could she find a person who'd gone into hiding? And who or what was Glynis running from?

And how could this mother leave her children in danger, if that was why she left town?

Maybe Kate was going to have to talk to the sheriff after all. Or perhaps Deputy Spencer.

With a discouraged sigh, she logged off the Internet and went downstairs. A woman was at the catalog terminal, and Livvy was checking out a stack of books for an elderly gentleman.

When he left with his armload of books, Kate asked Livvy, "What do you know about the foster-care system?"

Livvy put her glasses on top of her head. "Are you thinking of applying?"

"Not exactly. More like I'd like to know how it works."

"I had a neighbor in Nashville who had foster kids. A lovely grandmotherly type. She must have had half a dozen children come and go while we lived there."

"Did she ever take in three from the same family?"

Livvy shook her head. "Her house wasn't big enough. There are rules about how many bedrooms the family needs to have."

"Then sometimes the children from the same family are split up?"

"Oh yes, that can happen. My neighbor had two little brothers for a while. She used to take them on playdates to visit their older sisters and brother who were living with two other families. I thought it was terribly sad the children had to be apart."

So did Kate. Megan was right that she and her siblings might be separated if they had to go into the foster-care system. No wonder she didn't want Kate to contact the authorities.

The woman who'd been checking the catalog terminal came up to the counter.

"Thanks for the information," Kate said to Livvy, giving her friend a warm smile. "I'll see you at choir practice tonight."

Kate's next stop was the Town Hall. The architecturally undistinguished brick building across from the Town Green housed the offices of the mayor and city-council members as well as the sheriff's local office, where Skip Spencer was assigned.

The rain had washed the new leaves on the double row of maple trees that led up to the structure, and they glistened an almost Day-Glo green.

She entered through the double-glass doors and walked toward the deputy's office. Skip was at his desk, his chair tipped back and his feet propped on an open drawer, reading a magazine.

"Good morning, Skip."

The deputy's feet dropped to the floor with a bang. In his hurried effort to stand up, he nearly lost his balance. Waving his arms to regain his equilibrium, he sent the magazine sailing across the room, where it smacked into a portable whiteboard sitting in the corner.

"Hey, Missus Hanlon." He scurried after the magazine, his face almost as bright red as his hair. "You kinda startled me."

"I'm sorry." She swallowed a laugh. The twenty-five-year-old deputy was as earnest as could be, but there were times when he was as clumsy as a puppy who hadn't grown into his feet yet.

"The sheriff's not here right now. He's in Pine Ridge, at his office there. I can call him if—"

"That's all right, Skip. I'm hoping you'll be able to help me."

"Sure." He straightened his tan uniform shirt, brushing away an imaginary bit of lint. "What can I do for you?"

"I'm trying to locate a friend." Kate chose her words carefully. She didn't want to give away too much or alert the authorities, who might bring in children's services to check on the Maddock youngsters. "She moved away six weeks ago and didn't leave her new address. Is there any way you can track her down?"

"Well now, I'm not sure." He ran his hand along the back of his neck. "I could check to see if she's changed her address on her driver's license."

"That's a good idea." Although Kate didn't imagine Glynis would have officially moved to Nashville, leaving her children behind in Copper Mill.

Eager to please, Skip sat down at his desk and typed some commands on his computer keyboard. "What's your friend's name?"

"Glynis Maddock." She spelled it for him.

A few more keystrokes, and he brought up another screen. "This shows a Glynis Maddock residing in Knoxville. Age forty-two. Blonde hair, blue eyes. Five foot six, one hundred and twenty pounds. Is that your friend?"

Kate peered over his shoulder to examine the blurred photo of Glynis. The resemblance to the children was unmistakable. Kate mentally made a note of the family's former address in Knoxville.

"Yes, she's the one. But that's not her current address. She's been living out in Smoky Mountain Hollow for several years."

"Oh, then she definitely should've changed her address with the Department of Motor Vehicles. That's the law, you know."

"I'm sure it's just an oversight on her part," Kate said, nodding. "Is there any other way you can track down someone?"

"I can check for a police record, although I'm sure any friend of yours wouldn't have one. But if for some odd reason she does have a record, it'd show her last known address, a list of criminal associates, and outstanding warrants."

"I don't think she has a record, but go ahead. Take a look."

His fingers addressed the keyboard again. After a delay, the screen filled with data. Idly, he rubbed his slightly crooked nose as he read the information.

"Nope, no police record in Tennessee. I could check with other states, but that would take a few days."

"No, that won't be necessary."

He swiveled in his chair to face Kate. "Where was your friend headed?"

"To Nashville."

"If it's somethin' serious, I could notify the Nashville PD to be on the lookout for her. Was she driving a car?"

Kate didn't know. She hadn't asked Megan. And she was reluctant to sic the Nashville police on Glynis. "I think she was traveling with a friend. Hank Weller. Can you look him up?"

"Sure thing." He turned back to his computer.

Kate wasn't at all sure that Skip should be giving her this information. But he didn't seem concerned, so she wouldn't be either. Another one of those pluses for living in a small town. People trusted each other.

"I've got a Perry Weller who did time for armed robbery of a couple of convenience stores in Knoxville a few years back. Is he the one?"

She studied the booking photo on the screen. Perry Weller was a heavyset man with dark hair and several days' worth of whiskers. He stared at the camera sullenly, his expression giving Kate a cold shiver down her spine.

"I'm not sure." Kate wondered if Perry and Hank could be related. If so, Glynis could be in very bad company, running away from even worse company.

Swiveling around again, Skip said, "I'm sorry, Missus Hanlon. I don't know where else to check."

Skip hadn't come up with much useful information, and Megan might not know much about her mother's friends, but Kate decided that perhaps a former neighbor in Knoxville might have some answers. She hoped that Glynis had been friendlier toward her previous neighbors, and that not all of them had moved away in the intervening years.

THE FOLLOWING MORNING, Paul took the children to school, and Kate headed off for the hour drive to Knoxville. She knew it might be a waste of her time, but she was ready to try anything to locate Glynis.

She found the address on Glynis' driver's license, an apartment in a long, dreary row of six-unit apartment buildings. The street was mostly empty. The little patches of lawn in front of the units were poorly kept and muddy from the recent rain. A nearby playground featured broken asphalt and swings that looked equally decrepit.

The Maddock family had suffered hard times for longer than just a few years. Kate prayed for the children and that something helpful would come of her trip.

Cautiously, Kate walked up to the apartment where Glynis and her children had once lived, checking her surroundings as she went. She knocked. While she waited, she sensed that someone was watching her.

Surreptitiously, she glanced around. A curtain moved in a window opposite Glynis' apartment, but no one appeared.

Kate moved on to the next apartment and knocked again.

Almost to her surprise, a buxom woman with a scarf tied around her head swung open the door.

"Who're you?"

"I'm a friend of Glynis Maddock. I'm trying to locate her—"

"Don't know nobody like that." The woman glanced up and down outside her apartment, shook her head, then slammed the door shut.

Kate tried a couple more doors but got no answers. Yet she'd seen the curtains move on the opposite building a second time. A nosy neighbor, she decided, might be the most likely to have known Glynis. She walked across the unkempt patch of grass and knocked on that door.

She waited quietly, and when there was no answer, she knocked again. "I'm a friend of Glynis Maddock," she said to the closed door. "I think she may be in trouble, and I'd—"

The door whipped open, bringing with it a powerful whiff of tobacco. A gray-haired woman no taller than five feet, who could have been anywhere from sixty to eighty-five years old, glared out at Kate behind huge, oversized glasses with pink plastic frames.

"You shouldn't be askin' nothin' about Glynis. You keep away from here. You hear me? Keep away."

"Please. I have her children, and they need—" The door slammed closed.

Kate pulled a small notepad from her handbag and jotted down her name and phone number. Whoever this woman was, she knew something about Glynis. And knew she was in danger. Kate sensed that deep in her psyche.

Knocking again, Kate said, "I'm going to leave you my

phone number. If you know how to reach Glynis, please let her know that her children are all right. They miss her."

Only silence greeted her plea.

With a sigh, Kate sent up yet another prayer. If God had a plan for how she should help the children reunite with their mother, it wasn't clear to Kate. Yet.

She tucked the note she'd written into the doorjamb and hoped for the best.

IN COPPER MILL, Paul parked his truck in front of Town Hall and walked toward the entrance. He'd spent the morning going over some old sermons, and then he'd gotten a call from Deputy Spencer asking that Paul and Sam meet with him after lunch.

As he pulled open the glass door into the building, Paul heard Sam call to him.

"Hey, wait up." Breathing hard, Sam hurried up the steps to where Paul waited for him. "What's this meeting with Skip all about?"

Paul shrugged. "I figured it was about the vandalism, but Skip didn't say. I thought you'd asked to meet with him."

"Nope. But I'd sure like to stop those vandals. Maybe Skip has a lead on them."

Together they turned down the hallway to the deputy's office. When they entered the office, Skip snapped to attention in front of a portable whiteboard on rollers. Across the top of the whiteboard the deputy had written Operation Vandal Trap in purple letters. Below that heading was the word *Strategy* in red, followed by several items written alternately in green and blue.

"Good. You're both here right on time." Skip extended his hand to each of them in turn.

Paul eyed the whiteboard. "Guess you've come up with a plan to catch Sam's vandals."

"Right. No general would take his troops into the field without a battle plan. I've been working out the logistics of our operation and the supplies we'll need. The timing too, and the big guns we'll bring to bear on the miscreants."

Paul felt as though his number had come up in the lottery and he was about to be drafted into some trigger-happy general's army.

Sam studied the board and scratched at his sideburns. "Are you sure you haven't gone a little overboard, Skip?"

"Not at all. I've given this operation a lot of thought. Let me explain." Skip picked up a long stick to use as a pointer. He tapped the end on the first item listed below *Strategy*. "First we need to lure the vandals into action. We're going to *seed* the Dumpster behind your store with such tempting trash that the vandals won't be able to stay away."

Sam didn't seem fully impressed, nor was Paul. "Let's say we do lure the vandals to the Dumpster again, what happens next?"

"Right." Skip tapped the board with his pointer again. "This is when we turn on the floodlights we've rented from A1 Rentals in Pine Ridge. We'll light up the alley like it's noon in the middle of summer."

"Has the sheriff given you a budget to rent floodlights?" Paul asked.

Skip looked a bit sheepish. "I'm working on that, okay? The point is, we've got a plan and a strategy. What's going to happen after the lights go on is that two gates, one at either end of the alley, will be slid into place, cutting off the vandals with no means of escape. We'll have 'em trapped in a pincer movement from both ends of the alley at once."

Shaking his head, Sam sat down on the edge of Skip's desk. "There aren't any gates at either end of the alley, Skip. Where're you gonna get those?"

"I haven't quite worked that out yet, but I will." He grabbed hold of the whiteboard and tried to flip it over to the other side. "Let me show you the layout of the alley I've drawn. Every Dumpster is marked, and so are the security lights."

"This is a very interesting plan," Paul said, "and I know you've worked hard to come up with it. But I think in this case, the simpler the better."

Skip's freckled face pulled into a frown. "What do you mean?"

"He means we lie in wait for those juvenile delinquents on a dark night and scare the stuffin' out of them when they show up," Sam explained.

"That's pretty much what I had in mind," Paul agreed.

"Oh." Skip sounded dejected. "Okay. Well, I thought it was a good idea."

"It is, Skip," Paul said. "A stakeout is a great idea."

Chapter Nine

By Saturday, Kate had run out of leads to follow. As far as she could tell, Glynis had vanished into thin air. Kate knew she'd have to file a formal missing-person's report soon. The children couldn't be left in limbo forever. Eventually, children's services would have to get into the mix.

But not yet. Kate was determined to treat the girls to a day of pampering at Betty's Beauty Parlor. Or rather, it was Betty and her cohorts who had generously offered to give the Maddock children the royal treatment.

"I don't wanna be made over," Beck complained.

Paul ruffled the boy's hair. "You're just going to get a haircut, buddy. Then you and I are going to a baseball game down in Chattanooga."

The boy's eyes widened. "A *real* baseball game?"

"Yep. The Chattanooga Lookouts. They're a Double-A team, but they've got some pretty good players." Paul ushered Beck out the front door. "We'll ride in the truck and let the girls have the car."

Megan and Gwen were only a little less reluctant than Beck about a makeover, but they dutifully climbed into the car.

"What are they gonna do to us?" Gwen asked from the backseat.

"I imagine Betty or one of the other gals will start you both with a shampoo and rinse, and then trim your hair."

"I washed my hair last night." Megan snapped her seat belt in place. "Ma's the only one who's ever cut our hair."

Kate backed the car out of the garage. Because of the note she'd found in the trailer and the possible danger the children might be in, she'd made it a point to start checking for any unfamiliar cars or people lurking in the neighborhood before she left the house. A simple precaution, she told herself. So far there'd been no sign of an imminent threat.

"You'll love having a beautician cut your hair. And after your hair is styled, they'll give you a facial."

"A *facial*?" Clearly concerned, Gwen scrunched up her nose. "I don't need a new face. I like the one I've got."

"I do too, sweetie. Especially your cute little turned-up nose." Kate smiled into the rearview mirror. "But you'll love the facial, I promise. Maybe Betty can do a little makeup for you. Nothing too grown-up, of course. And fingernail polish and a pedicure. How does that sound?"

"It sounds expensive," Megan said softly.

"Don't worry." She patted the girl's arm. "It's a special gift from Betty. And after we're all done getting pampered and prettied up, we girls will go on a little shopping spree at the SuperMart in Pine Ridge." If Kate did have to eventually send the children off to foster care, she wanted them feeling better about themselves than they ever had before.

Located two doors down from the Mercantile, Betty's Beauty Parlor occupied a small storefront with a plate-glass window decorated with faded posters of women sporting various hairdos.

The bell tinkled when Kate opened the door, and they all went inside, with Beck and Paul trailing behind.

"This place is for *girls*," Beck announced in a stage whisper that reached the back of the shop, where Betty was combing out a customer's hair.

"Hey, Kate." She waved the comb in Kate's direction. "Tell that handsome young guy that the best lookin' men in town get their haircuts here. I don't give 'em girlie haircuts either."

Skeptical, Beck looked up at Paul for confirmation.

"She'll take good care of you, buddy. Get that long hair out of your eyes so you can see the baseball players better."

Kate urged the children to a padded-vinyl bench by the window where they could wait, but before she sat down with them, Renee Lambert called to her.

"Kate, dear, who are those little ragamuffins you've got with you?"

Trying not to grimace, Kate smiled back at her. "They're friends of ours who are staying with us for a while."

Ronda, one of Betty's stylists apparently yanked too hard on Renee's hair, and she cried out. "Ouch! Do be careful, Ronda!"

Renee's distress roused Kisses from his tote, and his little head popped up.

Gwen tugged on Kate's arm. "Miz Hanlon, is that a dog she's got?"

"Yes it is. His name is Kisses, and he goes everywhere with

Mrs. Lambert." Unless Renee dropped the dog off for Kate to babysit, which happened more often than Kate cared to think about.

"Can I go pet him?" Gwen whispered.

"We can ask." Taking the girl's hand, Kate led her to Renee's chair. "This is Gwen Maddock, Renee. She saw Kisses and wondered if she could take a closer look."

"Well, now, I don't know, dear." Renee eyed Gwen with considerable reluctance. "You know Little Umpkins doesn't always like—"

Before Renee could say no, Kisses took matters into his own hands . . . or paws. He popped up again and gazed at Gwen with his big brown eyes. She gingerly reached for him, and he licked her hand.

"Oh, isn't he cute," Gwen cooed as she scratched him on the top of his head. "I love him. He's so tiny."

Renee's sense of pride overcame her hesitancy. "Well, yes. He's a teacup Chihuahua. You won't see many as sweet as my Little Umpkins."

Before Kate knew what was happening, Beck had joined the coo-and-adore party for Kisses. The dog ate up all the attention. So did Renee.

From the doorway, Paul looked on with amusement. Kate wasn't too sure he felt any more at ease in the beauty shop than Beck.

Betty announced that she was ready for Beck. "Come on, young man. Let's see what a handsome devil you are under-neath all that gorgeous hair."

"Boys aren't gorgeous," he insisted.

"They are to me, darlin'."

By the force of her personality, Betty swept Beck back to the shampoo room and out of sight. A moment later, Alicia, who was stationed at the third chair in the salon, was ready for Megan.

"I don't want it cut too short," Megan protested.

Tall, with hair that rippled in dark waves halfway down her back, Alicia smiled and ran her fingers through the teenager's hair. "I wouldn't dream of cutting off too much. To think you were born with hair just like sunshine. I know women who would kill to have this color hair."

Megan grinned and blushed with embarrassment. "Well, I *hope* they don't kill me for a hank of my hair."

Kate couldn't help but feel sad for the girl's literal interpretation of the phrase. With a father in jail for murder, the word *kill* took on a much more personal meaning for Megan than it normally would for a thirteen-year-old.

"No, sweetie, I promise they won't." Alicia sat Megan in her chair, turning her toward the mirror and lifting Megan's long hair off her shoulders. "But the boys will sure take notice when I trim it up a bit and give you a soft, conditioning rinse."

Betty reappeared with Beck, who now wore a black nylon cape around his shoulders. He climbed up into Betty's chair, formed fists with both his hands, and made a macho face into the mirror.

Kate smothered a laugh.

As Renee got up, it was Gwen's turn to head back to the shampoo room. She gave Kisses one last air smooch before following Ronda.

"What dear children." Renee hooked her tote over her arm. "Where are they from?"

"They're from Smoky Mountain Hollow, but their mother is . . . away for a while." As a minister's wife, Kate made it a point not to lie. Sometimes not telling the whole truth was the best she could do to keep that vow.

Taking Kate's arm, Renee urged her away from Megan and Alicia where they wouldn't hear the conversation.

"How could anyone leave those sweet youngsters?" she asked in a low whisper.

Kate exhaled and spoke softly. "I'm not sure."

Though Renee might lack many charming qualities, her intuition was razor sharp. "Did she desert them?" she asked with a quiet gasp.

"I'm honestly not sure."

"Well, where is she?"

"I don't know." Kate admitted, wishing she hadn't said anything about Glynis. "I'm trying to locate her. There may be a problem—"

"Surely Livvy can help you find the woman. She's a genius at working that computer of hers."

"I've already spent some time Googling at the library, but I'll talk to Livvy and see what other search tools might work." Kate decided she'd return to the library first thing Monday morning and enlist Livvy's help.

"There, you see?" Apparently deciding she'd done her good deed for the day, Renee told everyone good-bye and floated out the door, Kisses happily bouncing along in his tote.

Betty finished with Beck's haircut pretty quickly. Kate

resisted telling him how handsome he looked as he raced out the door with Paul, both of them eager to get to the baseball game.

Chuckling to herself, Kate followed Betty to the cramped shampoo room in the back of the shop to begin her own beauty treatment.

BY THE TIME the girls had their facials, pedicures, and manicures, Gwen was all giggles and Megan simply glowed. The light touch of makeup Alicia had applied gave Megan's face a radiant appearance and let the promise of the beautiful young woman she'd become show through.

Meanwhile, Gwen kept flourishing her blue fingernails, admiring them at arm's length.

"Shopping next, or do you want lunch first?" Kate asked.

"Shopping!" the girls chorused.

Laughing, Kate led them back to the car for the drive to Pine Ridge.

The SuperMart parking lot was filled with cars, and customers packed the aisles inside. Kate and her young charges made their way to the juniors' and girls' departments.

"I think two outfits apiece will do it," Kate said. "Pick out one that you'd like to wear to church tomorrow and the other for everyday school wear."

"We're going to church?" Gwen gaped.

Megan nudged her sister with her elbow. "Mr. Hanlon's the preacher, so we gotta hear him preach, right?"

Gwen shrugged, apparently unconcerned with her big sister's pronouncement. "I guess."

"While you girls are picking out a few things you like, I'll pick up a couple pairs of jeans and shirts for Beck. Then you can try your outfits on in the dressing room."

Kate left them on their own while she went to the nearby boys' department.

By the time Kate had picked up a pair of nice jeans and a pair of khaki cargo pants similar to those she'd seen the boys in town wearing, plus matching shirts, the girls had arms full of clothes to try on.

Megan first tried on a denim skirt that came just above her knees and a long-sleeved, pale blue knit top with a scooped neckline. When she stepped out of the dressing room to show Kate, she smiled.

"You're beautiful," Kate said.

Megan's hair was pulled back on both sides and held up with pretty clips Alicia had given her. The style made her Wedgwood blue eyes stand out and revealed her perfect oval face.

Right then, a boy about Megan's age trudged by with his mother. He halted abruptly. "Megan?"

"Hey, Boyd."

"Wow. You look . . . pretty."

A blush colored Megan's cheeks as she gave him a shrug that said 'high time you noticed.' "Thanks" was all she said.

Walking backward, not able to take his eyes off Megan, Boyd bumped into a rack filled with frilly clothes. He blushed, turned, and fled in the direction his mother had gone.

"I think that outfit is a keeper," Kate said. "What do you think?"

Megan smiled shyly. "Can I wear it to church tomorrow?"

"Of course you may."

Gwen picked out an ankle-length, flower-print cotton skirt and a knit top for church. Both girls got new jeans and summery tops for school wear.

Kate wished she could buy them dozens of new outfits. The happy glow in the girls' eyes and the smiles on their faces as they proudly carried their packages out to the car made it all worthwhile.

Back at the Hanlon house, both Megan and Gwen settled down at the dining table. Megan created a cornhusk cowboy on a horse. Working quietly beside her sister, Gwen began drawing a mountain scene with crayons on the big sheet of paper Paul had given her for a kite.

It was almost dinnertime when Kate heard the sound of Paul's truck in the garage, and a moment later, Beck burst into the house.

"We won! We beat Huntsville! It was so cool. And I got to eat *two* hot dogs and caramel corn and a Coke, and then I puked. But I'm fine now."

Kate smiled despite her lurching stomach. "So you had a really good time, huh?"

"Yeah! It was great." He looked up at her from beneath the bill of a new red and white Chattanooga Lookout baseball cap with a grin so broad it nearly reached his ears.

Unable to resist, Kate pulled Beck into her arms and gave him the biggest hug she could muster. *Thank you, Father, for giving all the Maddock children a special day to remember.*

JUST BEFORE KATE DRIFTED OFF TO SLEEP that night, she bolted upright in bed.

Paul came awake instantly. "What's wrong?"

"I've been researching *Hank* Weller."

"Who's Hank Weller?" he asked groggily.

"Glynis' boyfriend. The one she went to Nashville with. But his name's probably not Hank."

"It's not?"

"No. I'd bet on it. I should have been looking for *Henry* Weller. Hank is a nickname."

"If you say so, honey." He tugged her back down next to him. "G'night."

A moment later, he was softly snoring, but Kate's mind whirled. Now she had even more fodder for her research Monday morning at the library. If Kate could find Henry Weller, with Livvy's help, perhaps Glynis would be with him. Then the children could reunite with their mother.

That thought tightened Kate's throat and caused tears to burn in her eyes. In a very short time, she'd come to love those three youngsters. She'd miss having them around.

It seemed impossible that the children's father, a man capable of committing murder, and their mother, who'd left them unsupervised for weeks, could produce such beautiful offspring, both inside and out.

Surely the Lord had a hand in that.

Chapter Ten

From her seat in the choir, Kate kept an eye on Megan, Gwen, and Beck where they sat together on an oak pew near the front of the church. Renee, bless her heart, had begged off of her choir responsibilities to take charge of the youngsters. She sat with them, helping them find the correct hymns in the hymnal and the appropriate responsive readings.

The children were all wearing their new clothes, their hair freshly trimmed and neatly combed, their faces washed. It was enough to make any mother proud. Too bad Glynis wasn't there to see them.

Granted, Beck had done some restless squirming during the sermon, but overall they'd been well behaved. Kisses seemed particularly pleased to have Gwen nearby. He kept popping up in his tote to check that she was still there.

For the last hymn, the entire congregation rose and sang at full volume. Paul gave the final benediction and dismissed the congregation.

Kate exited the building and met the children as they came out the door. The sun had turned a cool morning into a lovely spring day. Only the top branches of the trees that skirted the parking lot moved in the light breeze.

"You kids were so great." Kate gave Beck and Gwen a hug and smiled at Megan. "I was proud of you all."

Beck jammed his hands in the pockets of his new jeans. "When are we gonna have lunch? I'm hungry."

Cupping the back of the boy's head, Kate stroked his newly trimmed hair. "Maybe we can talk Pastor Hanlon into taking us out to lunch."

Beck brightened at the prospect.

When Paul finished chatting with the departing members of the congregation, many of whom congratulated him on his sermon, he joined Kate and the children.

"We've had at least one request for lunch," Kate told him. "Should we go to the Country Diner?"

The Hanlons often had Sunday lunch at the diner, and many members of the congregation frequented the popular eating spot as well.

"I have a better idea." He grinned and winked at Kate. "Since our young house guests are all dressed up and we are too, why don't we go to the Bristol at the Hamilton Springs Hotel? We'll make it a special day."

His suggestion surprised Kate. The children had already been treated to one special day, but she wasn't about to turn down a chance to eat at the Bristol, the nicest restaurant in Copper Mill. The locals felt it was a bit citified, catering to wealthy tourists, but Kate enjoyed both the service and the sophisticated ambience.

"I'll vote yes," she said. "How about the rest of you?"

Megan's forehead furrowed. "That's a pretty fancy place."

"I'll go if they've got hamburgers." Beck shrugged.

"I'm sure they do, buddy," Paul said.

Once they were all in agreement, they piled into the Honda, the three youngsters squeezing into the backseat. Paul drove, and Kate took the passenger seat.

Built in the early 1900s and recently restored, the two-story Hamilton Springs Hotel was constructed of red brick. Evenly spaced windows glistened as the noontime sun glanced off the panes, producing a diamond effect that shot rays of silver across the gardens.

Quite a few cars were in the parking lot, including the sheriff's patrol car and Deputy Skip Spencer's official black-and-white SUV with the county logo on the side.

"Wonder what brings them here," Paul mused out loud.

Megan leaned forward between the seats to get a better view. "Maybe we shouldn't go in."

"Let's at least take a look. Maybe they're just enjoying a leisurely brunch," Kate said.

"Ma always told us to stay away from cops."

At Megan's worried tone, Kate glanced over her shoulder. "Nothing to worry about today. Sheriff Roberts is a very nice man."

Sliding back onto the seat, Megan didn't look convinced.

Kate had to wonder why their mother had warned her children to stay away from the police. Kate had encouraged her own children to trust police officers and go to them if they needed help.

Of course, if Glynis or her boyfriend were involved in

something illegal, that would be a good reason for her to tell the children to steer clear of the law.

Or maybe the children had another reason to avoid the police. Kate didn't want to believe they were involved in anything illegal, like Dumpster-diving. Still, Megan had been pretty desperate to take care of her siblings.

By the time they parked and were walking toward the hotel entrance, a small crowd had gathered on the grassy lawn to the left of the building. Kate spotted the sheriff as well as Sybil Hudson, the hotel's efficient general manager.

"Let's see what's going on," Paul suggested.

The children hung back, following well behind Paul and Kate as they joined the crowd of onlookers. The focus of attention was an electric service cart used by hotel maintenance personnel around the grounds. The front of the bright yellow cart had crashed into something and was creased almost as far back as the driver's seat. Sheriff Roberts and Skip Spencer were examining the vehicle.

"What happened?" Kate asked Sybil.

Sybil pushed her glasses up farther on her nose and shook her head. "Looks like the vandals who have been messing around in town hit us last night. They got into our trash bin, pulled the mess out onto the driveway, then took a joyride in that cart."

"How did they get it started?" It looked too heavy to have been pushed from the maintenance area to this part of the hotel grounds.

"The maintenance men were forever misplacing the key to the cart, so they started leaving it in the ignition. Somebody just hopped in, stepped on the accelerator, and off they went. You can be sure the policy on keys is about to change."

"It's a shame someone did so much damage. I hope your insurance will cover the repairs."

"It should." The hotel manager wore her hair in a knot at the back of her head, and strands were coming loose as though undone by the vandals' action. "I'll call my agent first thing in the morning."

Paul spoke up. "Sam, Skip, and I have been talking about setting a trap for those vandals. Guess we'd better get to it."

"If you catch them, I'll be first in line to press charges," Sybil said. "Vandals tearing up the hotel property doesn't help my bottom line one bit, and it makes the guests nervous about their own safety."

Kate could empathize with Sybil's problem. The entire town was beginning to worry that their homes or businesses would be attacked next. At least for this act of vandalism, the children had a solid alibi. They'd been sound asleep in the Hanlon household only a few feet away from Kate.

But that didn't mean they had an alibi for the Dumpster affair in town. Kate had no way of knowing where the children had been when that vandalism occurred.

Edging her way around the crowd, she tried for a closer look at the damaged cart. The front end was caved in so far, it would be surprising if no one had been injured. Ugly scratches marred the dashboard, and it looked as though the steering wheel had been bent at an odd angle. Because of the force of the crash? Probably. But who, or what, would have been reckless enough, or vindictive enough, to run the cart at full power into a tree?

In any case, the cart would be expensive to repair.

Paul sidled up beside her. "Word has it we have a nine-year-old who's starving and may soon blow away because he's so hungry."

"Oh dear. We wouldn't want that." Smiling, she hooked her arm through his. "Let's hope they can seat us quickly."

As they walked toward the wide double doors leading into the hotel, Kate noticed that the children did their best to skirt the crowd, staying as far away from Sheriff Roberts as they could.

THE NEXT MORNING, Kate found herself at the library's front door again when Livvy arrived to open up.

"I think I should get you your own personal key," Livvy said with a laugh as she unlocked the door. "More research today?"

"More research, same topic." Kate followed her friend inside. After being closed up tight all night, the library smelled a bit musty. "I'm trying to locate Glynis Maddock, the mother of the children who are staying with us."

Nodding, Livvy switched on the overhead lights. "Yes, you mentioned that the other day."

"I've already tried Google and found nothing. I thought I might have better luck if I enlisted your researching brainpower."

Livvy entered her private office and switched on the light. "Well, there is one program we might try. It helps locate various articles and other information sources that require a subscription to access. It's called LexisNexis."

"Sounds perfect. I knew you could help, Watson."

Livvy chuckled. "You got it, Sherlock. Come on in my office and we'll take a look."

Sitting down at her desk, Livvy tucked her purse into the bottom drawer, then swiveled around to face her computer. "Bring a chair around and tell me what you need."

While Kate dragged a chair into place, Livvy booted up her computer.

"What was the woman's name again?"

"Glynis Maddock. She left town with her boyfriend over six weeks ago, heading for Nashville. She hasn't been heard from since, and I'm worried that something's happened to her. I was hoping you might have a way to check accident reports or hospital admissions."

Livvy jotted Glynis' name on a piece of scratch paper. "If she's been gone that long, no wonder you're worried. Let me see what I can find."

Kate watched the computer screen as Livvy alternately typed instructions and used her mouse.

"I'm not getting any hits in Tennessee for Glynis Maddock. I could widen the search to include the surrounding states or go back farther than two months. Or maybe I've got the name spelled wrong."

Kate wondered if Glynis had reached Nashville and simply kept going. It would devastate the children to learn that their mother had indeed deserted them.

"Try Hank or Henry Weller. Maybe you'll hit something there."

Livvy's fingers moved over the keyboard again. "The boyfriend?"

"So I'm told."

"Here we go. I got a couple of hits on Henry Weller." A few more clicks brought up a new screen. Livvy leaned forward to read the words as she scrolled down. "Uh oh. I don't think this is going to be good news."

Kate's heart missed a beat. "What is it?"

"This is from the *Tennessean*, the Nashville newspaper, written, let's see"—Livvy nodded her head rapidly as if mentally counting—"seven weeks ago. 'Two fatalities were reported in a high-speed rollover accident on Interstate 24 near La Vergne last night. The driver was identified as Henry Weller of Knoxville. Identification of the female passenger, who'd been thrown from the car, was delayed pending notification of next of kin. Paramedics pronounced both victims dead at the scene.'"

Chapter Eleven

K ate covered her mouth with her hand to hold back a sob. *Please, God, don't let it be true.* But even as she sent up the prayer, she knew in her heart the Lord had already called Glynis home. *But the children, the poor children . . .*

Livvy turned away from the computer. "I'm sorry, Kate. This will be terrible news for the children."

"I know." Her throat tightened with sorrow. She blinked back tears. *How can I tell them?* "Do you think there's a way I can confirm it really was Glynis and not someone else?"

You'd have to talk to the highway-patrol officer in charge of the accident investigation."

"All right." With an effort, Kate pulled herself together. "Then that's what I'd better do. Thank you for your help, Livvy."

Livvy squeezed Kate's hand. "Sorry it wasn't better news."

"Not your fault."

As Kate reached the library front counter, Jennifer McCarthy came bustling through the front door. A recent graduate of the University of Tennessee, she was a hard-working reporter for the *Copper Mill Chronicle*.

"Hey, Mrs. Hanlon. You got any hot church news for me today?"

"Unfortunately not today."

Livvy stepped behind the counter. "Kate just found out some sad news, I'm afraid."

Jennifer's eyebrows rose marginally. "I'm sorry. What happened?"

Kate sensed Jennifer's reporter instincts had kicked into high gear. She had to be careful or Glynis' story could end up on the front page of the *Chronicle*.

"There was an auto accident near Nashville," Kate said cautiously. "An acquaintance of mine was killed."

"Recently?"

"Almost two months ago." Glancing around, Kate tried to think of a gracious way to escape the reporter's prying.

"I'm really sorry. I have to go." She waved to Livvy as she hurried out of the library, the weight of the children's grief already on her shoulders.

She wished Paul were there with her, but he was visiting Pine Ridge Hospital this morning in his role as chaplain.

Letting herself into the parsonage, she was struck by the silence and the scattered evidence of children living there. Beck's bed in the living room. A schoolbook left behind and a dirty milk glass on the kitchen counter.

She found a pen and notepad and dialed information to get the number of the highway-patrol office in Nashville. When an officer answered with a brisk "Highway Patrol," she explained who she was and asked to speak to the person in charge of the accident that killed Henry Weller.

The wait seemed extremely long as she doodled stars and flowers on the yellow notepad.

"Captain Sanchez," a male voice barked into the phone. "Who's this?"

She gave him her name and identified herself as the pastor's wife at Faith Briar Church in Copper Mill, a role that usually provided her with some credibility.

"I'm calling about a fatal accident nearly two months ago that took the life of Henry Weller. I believe the woman with him was Glynis Maddock."

There was a pause, and Kate pictured the captain searching through paperwork or checking his computer.

The captain asked Kate for her name again as well as her address and phone number. Then he asked, "What is your relationship to the crash victims, Mrs. Hanlon?"

Kate's heart sank a little further. By asking that question, the captain had virtually confirmed Glynis was the deceased woman. "I've never met either of them, but Glynis' children are staying with me and my husband."

"You're not in Knoxville?"

"No sir. As I understand it, Glynis and her family moved from Knoxville to Copper Mill three years ago."

"I see. That's why we couldn't locate her next of kin at the address in Knoxville that was listed on her driver's license. She hadn't left a forwarding address."

Which suggested she might have been on the run then as well, Kate thought.

"Do you know if Ms. Maddock was involved in any illegal activities?" the captain asked.

"Not that I'm personally aware of. But as I said, I never met the woman." Recalling the handwritten note, she added, "It is possible she was running away from something or someone."

"What was Ms. Maddock's relationship with Mr. Weller?"

"Her daughter told me that Hank Weller was her mother's boyfriend." Kate paused. "Captain Sanchez, any information you can give me would be much appreciated. I need to know as much as I can in order to carefully and accurately break this horrible news to the children."

"You have custody of the children?"

"It's an informal arrangement," she hedged. "But I am taking care of them, yes."

Captain Sanchez seemed to ponder her request for a moment. "Okay, Mrs. Hanlon. The deaths of the two people in the car were a result of a high-speed chase by patrol officers. One officer had pulled the car over to cite the driver for speeding. The vehicle stopped, but when the officer got out of his car, the driver of the suspect vehicle slammed his car into reverse, pinning the officer against his own patrol car."

Kate gasped.

"After the suspect vehicle took off, our officer was able to get to his radio and report the incident. Other patrol cars went in pursuit of the suspect. In the course of that chase, the suspect's car flipped over . . . killing both occupants."

"Is your officer going to be all right?"

"We think so, ma'am."

"I'm glad to hear it." Despite the tragedy of Glynis' death, her biggest concern remained the children's safety. "I have to ask, Captain . . . Are the children in danger?"

"It's possible, Mrs. Hanlon. After identifying the suspect, we discovered that he was wanted for a series of armed robberies in Knoxville—several convenience stores and a jewelry store."

Who was Glynis that she had gotten involved with a thief?

"We've now been able to identify the two other men involved in the robberies. Henry's brother, Perry Weller"—Kate instantly pictured the dark-haired, heavyset man with the shadowed whiskers that Skip Spencer had shown her—"and Curt Smedley, both career criminals and considered armed and dangerous."

This was too much for Kate to take in at once.

"There's more. The merchandise stolen from the jewelry store, close to a hundred thousand dollars' worth of cut diamonds, hasn't been recovered yet. A few days after the accident, someone broke into our impound yard and vandalized what was left of the suspect's damaged vehicle. Ripped out the overhead lining, tore up the seats, and every place else where the stolen property might have been hidden. We think the doers were probably Weller's brother and his buddy Smedley."

"What are you saying, Captain?" She glanced out the kitchen window where everything looked so normal. A light breeze shifted the maple leaves. A blue jay pecked the ground for a hidden morsel to eat. In contrast, a painful knot had tied itself in Kate's stomach.

"We don't think they found what they were looking for. Our accident investigators had already removed the victims' personal effects and examined the car for contraband. The only thing they found was some old hamburger wrappers and a bag of marbles. Chances are good that Perry Weller and Curt Smedley will keep looking for the diamond stash. The next logical place would be where Henry Weller had been holed up before he got to Nashville. I'm guessing he was staying with Glynis Maddock."

"Yes, I've been told he was."

"Weller and Smedley are very dangerous, Mrs. Hanlon. If they get wind of where Hank was, they'll come searching for whatever he left behind." The man paused. "Have the children said anything about, I don't know, seeing any stolen property? Any suspicious characters hanging around their neighborhood?"

"Not at all, Captain. They're entirely innocent and very worried about their mother." But there had been someone—or something—in the woods the day she'd moved the children out of the trailer and brought them home with her. But realistically, the noise had probably been made by an animal or a neighbor passing through, and she'd been spooked for nothing.

"Yeah, I understand," the captain said. "This sort of thing is tough on kids."

An unbearable burden.

"I urge you to use the utmost caution, Mrs. Hanlon. These criminals may try to use the children to recover the diamonds they stole."

By the time Kate hung up, her hands were shaking and she had a sick feeling in her stomach.

It seemed clear that Hank had double-crossed his brother and their partner by taking the diamonds. Since the two crooks had not yet shown up in Copper Mill, Kate assumed they didn't know Hank's whereabouts. Yet it also seemed likely that the news of the accident had reached Hank's brother, leading him and Smedley to the Nashville impound yard.

With the police unable to publicly identify Glynis, the two crooks had likely hit a dead end in their search for the diamonds.

If Perry Weller and his buddy ever learned that Hank had been staying with Glynis, whatever danger the woman had tried to escape would land right smack on Kate's own doorstep.

Chapter Twelve

Her mouth as dry as day-old toast, Kate stared at the phone for several minutes before she could get her head around what she needed to do.

Finally she prayed out loud. "Dear Lord, give Glynis Maddock and Hank Weller peace in your loving arms. Lay your healing hands on the officer who was injured in the accident and help him to make a full recovery. Help the children—"

Her voice broke, and she swallowed the lump of sorrow she felt for the children. "Please comfort Megan, Gwen, and Beck, and help them be strong in the knowledge that you are with them even though their mother is no longer here on earth.

"And please, dear Lord, help me and Paul to ease their pain and grief, and give us the strength to support them as they face an uncertain future.

"I ask this in your name. Amen."

As Kate raised her head, she felt strengthened and ready to face what was to come.

First, she had to call Paul. She wanted him there when she brought the children home from school. Breaking the news of their mother's death would require them both to be strong and compassionate. That was Paul's forte.

She tried to call the sheriff, but he wasn't in. She left a message.

It was several hours before she'd have to pick up the children from school. She decided to use that time to search for the diamonds herself. If she could find the stashed loot and turn it in to the authorities, then Hank's brother and his partner would have no need to harm the children.

Moving quickly, Kate drove to Smoky Mountain Hollow and parked in front of the trailer where the car could be seen from the road. If the criminals came by, she didn't want them to think the place had been vacated.

Somehow the derelict trailer looked even more forlorn than it had the last time she'd been there. A shroud of grief seemed to have descended over it, making the decay more pronounced. The shadows in the silent woods that surrounded the place stood witness to the breakdown of both a home and a family.

If Hank Weller had a stash of diamonds, Glynis certainly hadn't benefited, and her connection to the man had cost her her life.

Cautiously, Kate climbed out of the car. Her heart lodged in her throat. What if Perry Weller had already tracked his brother back to Glynis' home? It had, after all, been nearly two months since the accident. But it still seemed unlikely that the men had found the trailer, since the children had been living there until recently and surely would have noticed two dangerous lurkers.

The sight of the turned-over trash can near the clothesline

drew her attention. No one had cleaned up the soggy mess, now partly dried by the sun.

Keeping alert for signs that someone had been there, she walked over and picked up a few scattered sheets of paper that had fallen from the can—a discarded test from school, a picture of a horse cut out of a magazine, an empty egg carton. There were also several wrappers from a fast-food drive-thru in Pine Ridge.

She tossed what she'd picked up back into the can, which was empty except for some coffee grounds and a soccer ball that had gone flat.

Shaking off the eerie feeling the silent woods created, she stepped up onto the trailer porch. The uneven wood creaked under her feet and shifted slightly.

Tentatively, she tried the doorknob. It turned in her hand. Megan had been right; the door didn't lock.

The living room was just as she and the children had left it. She was pretty sure no one had rummaged around inside since she'd taken the youngsters home with her.

Kate stood quietly for a moment considering where she might hide a stash of stolen diamonds. Not in the living room where the children might stumble across the loot. More likely the master bedroom. She headed down the narrow hallway to the back of the trailer. She bet that Hank would have hidden the loot on a high shelf in the closet, where the children wouldn't see it, and disguised it so that Glynis wouldn't know it was there.

The bed was made, an old blue quilt pulled up to two pillows. A pile of dirty laundry lay in a corner. Kate used her foot to shove the garments aside. No stash of diamonds there.

Opening the closet, she found only a few dresses hanging from the rack and a couple of men's shirts. Standing on tiptoe, she pulled down a shoe box from the top shelf. She checked the contents—old bills and receipts that she quickly flipped through.

Another box contained photos—family snapshots of Glynis, the children, and a man she took to be their father. There was even a photo of Glynis standing in front of a rustic cabin with another man whom Kate assumed was the late Hank Weller.

As Kate glanced through the photos, she smiled to see Megan as a towheaded toddler and later with cute pigtails and missing front teeth. She set the box aside to take with her. The children would want to keep the memories of their parents alive.

Not finding the diamonds in the closet, she checked the drawers in the built-in dresser. Once again she came up empty.

She tried the bed next. She looked under it, lifted the mattress to look underneath for a hiding place, and even pulled off the bottom sheet to see if someone had cut a hole in the mattress.

She tried the bathroom, looking inside a jar of cold cream, behind the toilet, and inside the water tank. The virtually empty freezer in the kitchen produced no diamonds in the ice-cube tray either. She tried to recall every crime show she'd seen on TV and every mystery novel she'd read, trying to remember where crooks hid evidence. Apparently she hadn't watched enough of those shows or read enough books because she found nothing incriminating. She discovered that Glynis' housekeeping wouldn't pass a white-glove test, but she drew a blank for stashed diamonds.

With a quick glance at her watch, she realized it was time to pick up the children. She dreaded telling them the news about their mother, but she had no choice. She prayed that God would give her the right words to bring comfort to the youngsters.

Picking up the box of snapshots, she left the trailer, closing the door firmly behind her.

As she reached her car, she got a prickly sensation on the back of her neck as though someone was behind her. She turned around, searching the woods for any sign of life.

Something cracked, a sound as loud as gunfire. She froze.

"Who's there?" she called.

No answer. Not even a bird stirred in the treetops.

Her heart thundering in her ears, she yanked open the car door, tossed the box of photos onto the passenger seat, and got out of there as fast as the Honda would take her.

AT THE SCHOOL, Megan claimed the front passenger seat while the younger children banged their way into the back.

"Hey." Megan picked up the box of photos so she could sit. "I recognize this. It's our pictures. Ma's gonna put 'em in a scrapbook someday."

Gwen poked her head between the two front seats. "Let me see."

Megan ignored her sister. "How'd you get these?"

"I was out at your trailer," Kate admitted.

"How come?"

"Buckle up everyone." Starting the car, Kate pulled away from the curb. "I wanted to see if anyone had been there."

"Was Ma there?" Beck asked hopefully. "Has she come back?"

Kate glanced into the rearview mirror. "I'm afraid not, honey." His down-turned lips and the way his gaze slid away nearly broke Kate's heart.

Megan sensed something was wrong. "What's going on?" she asked quietly.

"We'll talk when we get home."

The girl continued to stare hard at Kate, her blue eyes accusing, making the drive feel interminable. In the backseat, Gwen and Beck chattered away about a child who'd fallen off the climbing toy at recess and hurt himself. Megan remained sphinxlike.

To Kate's relief, when they arrived home, Paul's truck was in the garage. He met them at the door.

"Hey, gang," he said in greeting as the children went inside.

Kate reached up to give him a quick kiss. "Thanks for coming home early."

"The kids are going to need us both."

She nodded, her heart heavy in her chest. "Put your things away children, then come into the living room. We have something to tell you."

Megan was wide eyed. "It's bad isn't it?"

"Yes. I'm afraid so."

Tears immediately sprang to Megan's eyes, but she blinked them away and straightened her shoulders. "Come on, you guys. Put your stuff where it belongs."

Like a mother hen with her chicks, Megan rounded her siblings up and sat them down on the sofa, one on each side of her, her arms around their shoulders. She looked up at Kate with dread in her eyes.

Wanting to be near the children, Kate perched on the arm of the sofa by Gwen. Paul stood nearby.

Kate took a deep breath and began. "This morning I learned that your mother was in a serious car accident near Nashville."

"Is she all right?" Gwen asked.

Megan tugged the younger children even closer to her.

Kate's throat was tight with unshed tears for the children. "No, honey. I'm afraid your mother isn't all right. She was badly hurt, and she died."

Gwen and Beck turned to Megan, pleading with their eyes for her to deny the truth of Kate's pronouncement.

"Ma's gone. We won't ever see her again," Megan said.

The younger children burst into tears and buried their heads in Megan's chest. She held and petted them, stoically looking straight ahead and not shedding a single tear herself.

It was painful to watch the grief pouring out of the children and Megan's valiant effort to remain strong.

Kate reached across Gwen to stroke Megan's golden blonde hair. "It's all right to cry if you want. You don't have to hold it in."

Paul crouched down in front of Beck and placed a reassuring hand on the boy's back. "I'm sorry, buddy. You know, when something like this happens, I like to say a prayer. It helps me to not feel so alone or bad if I know God is with me. Would that be okay with you kids?"

The children appeared too stunned to respond, so Paul took their silence as acceptance.

"Dear Lord in heaven, it's hard to understand why you'd take a mother away from her children, but we know you had a good reason. Help Beck and Gwen and Megan to accept your solace and love as your Son urged children to come unto him.

"Make them strong in the knowledge that you will never desert them but will remain at their side to help them carry the burden of their grief. Be with them in the days and weeks ahead. We ask this in Thy name. Amen."

Megan's eyes filled with unshed tears, and her chin quivered. "What's going to happen to us?"

"For now, you're going to stay right here with us," Kate said. "Things will work out. You'll see."

The children continued to sob in Megan's arms. "We don't have anyplace to go," she said.

"Do you know how to reach your father?"

"Ma didn't want us to write to him or anything." The young teen swallowed hard. "When he went to jail, Ma divorced him. Said he'd be in prison for so long that we'd be grown up before he got out, and she'd be an old woman."

"Do you know which prison?" Kate asked.

Megan shook her head.

"What's your father's name?"

"Wyn. He went to prison so long ago, Gwen and Beck don't even remember him."

"I'll find out where he is," Kate promised.

Even if he was a killer who'd been locked up for life, he might lead Kate to a relative who could take the children in and care for them. She might have tried to locate the children's father earlier, but she'd been too focused on Glynis' whereabouts . . . not the search for a convicted murderer.

Now the situation had changed.

DINNER WAS A SUBDUED AFFAIR. No one had much of an appetite. When bedtime rolled around, the younger children went willingly, their eyes still red-rimmed from crying. Megan was about to go to bed too, when Kate asked her to come sit with her on the sofa.

"I'm so sorry about your mother."

Exhaling a long sigh, Megan lifted her shoulders in a defeated sigh. "I prayed, but I guess God didn't hear me."

"Oh, honey, it's so hard to explain why bad things happen. The Lord must have wanted your mother up in heaven with him, but we may never understand the reason why."

Megan didn't look any more convinced now than she had been when Paul had prayed with the children.

"Megan, I need to ask you some questions about Hank Weller. Did he ever seem secretive?"

"Sometimes, I guess. He'd go off for a day or two and come back smelling like booze."

"Did you ever see him hiding anything that he didn't want you to see?"

"Like what?"

"Something small. A bag or a small box."

She shook her head. "I don't think so. I just tried to stay away from him as much as I could. The other kids too. He gave us the creeps."

Kate could understand that, but it didn't help her locate the missing diamonds. Only when she did that and turned them over to the authorities would she feel confident that the children were safe from Hank's brother and his associate.

LATER THAT EVENING, Kate logged onto her home computer, with its slow dial-up connection, to do some Internet sleuthing. Surely the Tennessee prison system had a way to locate a prisoner.

Two hours later, she turned off the computer without having discovered Wyn Maddock's location. She'd typed his name on a form at the Department of Corrections Web site, but all she'd gotten was a Not Found response. She didn't have his TOMIS ID number, which seemed to be the key to tracking down an individual prisoner among the nineteen thousand incarcerated in the state.

It was possible, of course, that he'd already been released from prison, but she didn't think that would have happened if he'd been convicted of murder.

More than likely, she had his name spelled wrong. Maybe like Hank, Wyn was a nickname. But a nickname for what?

Kate turned off the lights and crawled into bed beside Paul. Resting her head on his shoulder, tears leaked out of her eyes for the sweet children she'd come to love. She brought her husband up to date on what she had learned—and not learned—about Hank Weller and his criminal partners, and the missing diamonds.

"You'd better leave things to the sheriff, Katie. These men you're talking about could be dangerous."

"I know. But with the children involved, I don't think I can stop searching for answers."

Chapter Thirteen

The children were late dragging themselves out of bed for breakfast. They looked completely worn out, their eyes still puffy from crying and their faces pale. Kate hadn't slept well either and had risen early to spend time reading her Bible. That had comforted her.

Sitting at the head of the table, Paul was just eating his last bite of the pancakes Kate had made as a treat for them all.

"Looks like you had a long night," he commented gently to the children.

Megan managed a shrug. Gwen and Beck simply stared glumly at their glasses of orange juice.

Kate carried a plate of pancakes to the table and sat down. "Would you like to stay home from school today?"

"Can we?" Enthusiastic about the idea, Beck reached for the pancakes.

Hearing no objections from the others, Kate proposed an idea that had come to her during the night. "I think it would be a good day for you to remember the happy times you and your family had together. I have a scrapbook I was going to use for one of my grandchildren, and I've never gotten around to putting anything in it. You could use the snapshots I found at the trailer and draw pictures about the fun things you did together."

"It wouldn't change anything," Megan said. "Ma's still gone."

"Yes, she's gone," Paul said. "But as long as you hold her in your hearts, she'll be alive to you. Remembering the good times will ease the hurt you're feeling."

Kate hoped that would be true, but she had an ulterior motive too. She wanted a chance to ask more questions about their past and their father without alerting them to the fact she hadn't been able to locate him. The pictures themselves might hold some clue to his whereabouts.

Breakfast didn't improve the children's somber mood much.

After Paul helped Kate clear the table, she brought out the scrapbook, crayons, colored paper, scissors, and glue. Megan got the box of photos.

"There's an ecumenical luncheon today in Chattanooga I'm supposed to attend," Paul told Kate. "If you need me here, I can skip it."

"No you go ahead. We'll be fine. I'm going to call the school principal to let her know what's happened and that the children are here with us."

"Good idea."

A few minutes later, dressed in a dark suit and tie, he told them all good-bye and promised to get back home as early as he could.

The children didn't seem to know how to begin on the scrapbook, so Kate made a suggestion. "Why don't you put the pictures in order, the oldest ones first and then the newer ones spread out across the table."

Megan dumped out the pictures and spread them around like domino pieces.

"Here's one of Becker when he was a baby. He's bald!" Gwen giggled.

"I wasn't bald," Beck insisted.

Megan glanced at the snapshot and sent a superior look toward her sister. "That's you, squirt. You're wearin' pink pajamas. They dress boy babies in blue."

"That's me?" She seemed astonished to see her own baby picture.

Reaching across the table, Kate checked the back of the photo, noting the date stamp. No other identification was listed.

"What year were you born?"

"I dunno," Gwen said.

"Well, you're ten years old, right?" Kate questioned. "So your birth year was—"

Gwen quickly did the math.

"Then this must be your picture," Kate concluded, showing her the date stamp. "Beck wasn't born yet. You were adorable."

Gwen blushed and studied the picture more carefully.

Getting up on his knees, Beck shoved the pile of snapshots around. "Where's my baby picture?"

"I'm sure there's one there somewhere," Kate said.

As the youngsters tried to make some order out of the snapshots, Kate managed to get their birthdates and jotted them down.

"Were y'all born in Knoxville?" she asked.

"I was born in Kentucky," Megan said. "Someplace called Sulphur Well."

"*Eww*, sounds stinky." Beck pinched his nose.

Kate smothered a laugh. At least this project gave the children something to think about besides their mother's death.

"Did your parents get married in Sulphur Well?" she asked.

"I dunno. Ma never said," Megan replied.

"Do you know your mother's maiden name?" Kate asked.

Shaking her head, Megan continued to arrange the pictures on the table. "Ma never said. I know her ma died before I was born."

Kate thought it sad that the children had never known the special love their grandparents could have given them.

"Megan, do you know if your mother had copies of your birth certificates?"

Megan didn't know the answer to that either. Or if Wyn was a nickname for something else. Or where he was born. Clearly the Maddock family hadn't kept close track of their records or their family tree.

Kate scanned the photos for some other clue. Megan had set aside the picture of Glynis and Hank in front of a small log cabin.

"Where was that picture taken?" Kate asked out of curiosity.

Glancing briefly at the photo, Megan shrugged. "Someplace on Tellico Lake. Ma didn't have a very good time. She said Hank spent all day arguing with his brother, so she came home early."

An argument between thieves, Kate suspected. That was one picture that wouldn't go into the family album.

A picture of Gwen's fifth-birthday party suggested they were living in the run-down Knoxville apartment building

Kate had visited. But there was an earlier snapshot of a small house on a grassy lot in the woods. According to Megan, the family had been living there when Beck was born. She didn't remember the address but thought it was in Knoxville, or nearby. Perhaps after Wyn had gone to prison, Glynis had been forced to move somewhere less expensive.

Kate was becoming more discouraged by the moment. Picking up a fairly recent snapshot of the children, she smiled at how happy they looked, and felt her heart break a little more for the loss of their mother.

"Would you mind if I kept this snapshot of the three of you?" Kate asked.

Megan gave an indifferent shrug. "Sure, if you want to."

When the children had the pictures sorted more or less chronologically, Kate asked them to tell her their favorite memory of their mother.

"Ma used to take me to the park and push me on the swings," Beck said.

"When I was little, Ma sewed me a blue sundress that she said matched my eyes," Gwen contributed.

Megan remained silent for a moment, her gaze focused on one of the snapshots that included Glynis. "I liked it when she brushed my hair."

Again, Kate's heart went out to the youngsters, and she vowed to brush Megan's hair every chance the girl would allow.

Her voice broke when she spoke. "All . . . right. You're all such good artists, why don't you draw a picture of your favorite memories, and you can put those in the scrapbook too."

Soon after they started working on their pictures, the door-bell rang. Kate grimaced as she went to answer the door. She really didn't want to deal with any added problems just now.

As soon as she opened the door, Renee, dressed in a bright pink jogging outfit, swept into the room. "Oh, good, you're home. Mother is driving me crazy, and I was hoping—" She stopped when she saw the children. "Is this a school holiday?"

"No." Kate hooked Renee's arm through hers. "I let the kids stay home today," she whispered. "Yesterday we learned that their mother died in a car accident almost two months ago. They're understandably—"

"Oh, my sweet little dears!" Her hand covering her heart as though she might swoon, Renee ran tippy-toed across the moss green shag carpeting to the kitchen table, her tote sway-ing from her arm. There she began kissing and hugging the youngsters, wailing about how sorry she was for their loss.

Beck seemed a little nonplussed by her exuberant over-ture, but the girls didn't appear to mind.

Following Renee to the table, Kate felt a bit overwhelmed herself. While she was grateful for the older woman's con-cern, Renee came off more like a tornado blowing through the house than a sympathetic friend.

When her oohing and aahing finally slowed down, Kate said, "Was there something you wanted, Renee?"

"Oh dear, it was nothing. I was simply going to ask you to babysit Kisses while I went for a massage. He's not fond of the aromatherapy I prefer. But I can see your duty is to console these poor, poor youngsters, so I won't impose on you."

Gwen piped up. "I can babysit Kisses. Please. I love Little Umpkins. He won't be any trouble, I promise." She looked to Kate hopefully.

Kate's inclination to roll her eyes at Renee's antics nearly got the better of her.

Instead, Kate simply nodded. "I'm sure the children would love to have Kisses stay here for an hour or two." *No more than that*. Although she had to admit, having an animal to cuddle might be good for Gwen.

"Oh, you're a lifesaver, Kate. You too Gwen, sweetie." She handed Gwen the tote with Kisses in it. "I'll just fetch his lunch from the car. Of course, you'll have to cook it for him."

She scurried out to her car and back again in seconds, handing Kate a plastic container of whatever it was that made up Kisses' lunch.

"Now don't serve it to him too hot," she warned. "We wouldn't want him to burn his pink little tongue."

"Of course not," Kate mumbled.

The rest of the morning went surprisingly well. The children alternated turns holding and fussing with Kisses and working on their drawings, which were both artistic and touching. Megan took charge of arranging the contents of the scrapbook. She labeled the photos and mounted them on colored paper that she shaped using Kate's pinking shears.

By midafternoon, Renee reappeared, apparently invigorated by her massage followed by a leisurely lunch at the hotel.

She oohed and aahed over the children, their scrapbook, and Kisses, then swept the dog up in his tote and was gone.

Kate exhaled an exhausted breath. That woman could wear out a marathon runner!

By the time Paul got home, the children were restless. Kate sent them outside to play, admonishing them to stay close by.

Paul slipped off his suit jacket and loosened his tie. "How are they doing?"

"Amazingly well, all things considered."

"Kids can be pretty resilient. There'll still be some bad moments, I'm sure."

"I know." Somehow she would have to make permanent arrangements for the children, plus deal with the trailer and what Glynis had left behind. "I've been trying to track down their father."

"I thought you said he's in jail."

"That's what they told me. But I didn't have any luck finding him through the Department of Corrections Web site. I think it's because I don't have his name exactly right and don't know his prisoner ID. If you can stick around for a bit, I thought I'd go see if Livvy can help me check the children's birth records. Those should have the father's name on them. We're running low on milk again too."

"Sure, go ahead. I'll start dinner if you'd like."

She smiled and kissed him. "I knew there was a reason I married you."

She grabbed a lightweight jacket from the front closet and drove into town. The sky had turned pewter gray with the threat of rain, and the wind had begun to whip the tops of the trees along Main Street. She parked and walked into the library.

"Hey, Liv."

The librarian looked up from the magazine she was reading behind the front counter and lifted her glasses to the top of her head. "You definitely get points for being a frequent visitor to the library. What's up this time?"

"Same general topic. Can you check marriage licenses and birth records on LexisNexis? I'm trying to locate Glynis' ex-husband."

"Let's give it a try." Setting the magazine aside, Livvy came out from behind the counter. "Is he the father of the children?"

"I'm afraid so. Glynis Maddock was married to Wyn Maddock, who's supposed to be in prison. But I can't locate him online. I'm guessing I've got his name spelled wrong or that Wyn is a nickname for something else. So I thought if I could find the children's birth records, he'd be properly listed on those."

"Should be." In her office, Livvy sat down in front of the computer and brought up a new screen. "What county were they born in?"

"Two were born in Knoxville. Gwen and Becker Maddock."

"Okay I'll look there first. You have their birth dates?"

Kate provided the information and watched as the computer screen flashed from one set of information to another.

Livvy seemed to slow down, then start over again.

"That's strange," she said. "I can't find any record of a Maddock born on those dates in Knoxville. I've checked nearby counties, but there's nothing there either."

"That is odd." Kate pondered that for a moment. "The older girl was born in Kentucky, Sulphur Well. Can you see if there's a record for Megan Maddock there?"

Again, Livvy deftly brought up a new screen and typed in the information.

"Nope. Nothing there," she said, shaking her head.

Kate leaned back in her chair. "Well, those children didn't simply fall out of the sky and drop into Copper Mill. There has to be some record of them being born somewhere."

Livvy turned to Kate. "Could it be they were adopted? If it was a closed adoption, their names won't show up in the birth records. But I can try court records and see if they turn up under adoptions."

Kate didn't think Glynis, with her long-standing financial struggle, would have been a good prospect to adopt three children. Although during her marriage, the family income could have been higher.

"I'm not optimistic," Kate said, "but give it a shot."

Once again Livvy went to work on her computer and found nothing. "Maybe no birth certificate was issued. If the mother gave birth at home, that sometimes happens."

"But when the children enter school, don't they have to present something that says when they were born?"

Thoughtful, Livvy tucked a strand of her auburn hair behind her ear. "What else can we check?"

"There has to be some way to track down Wyn Maddock. Can you check for an arrest record?"

"Here in Tennessee?"

"At this point I'm not sure of anything, but I got the impression from his daughter that he was arrested in Knoxville. She said he murdered someone."

"How long ago?"

"They didn't know exactly. The youngest child is nine, and he doesn't know his father at all, so the crime that sent

Wyn Maddock to prison must have taken place about that many years ago."

While Livvy went back to work again, Kate glanced around the librarian's office. A recent copy of the *Copper Mill Chronicle* sat on the corner of her desk. One corner of the Nashville *Tennessean* stuck out beneath it.

"I'm finding a bunch of robberies and driving-under-the-influence arrests, including one drunk-driving fatality." Livvy scrolled down a screen. "Nothing about anyone named Wyn or Maddock. Let me check the Knoxville newspaper. Maybe they picked up the story."

After a few more minutes, Livvy turned away from her computer and shook her head. "I'm sorry, Kate. I can't find anything related to Wyn Maddock."

How could that be? "Do you suppose Glynis changed her name or was using a false identity? Maybe she went back to her maiden name."

"I don't know. Whatever she did, she doesn't show up in the records anywhere that I can find."

"Glynis did have a driver's license," Kate said, recalling Skip's database search. "That much I know. Other than that, I guess we've hit another dead end."

The only other explanation Kate could think of was that Glynis was in witness protection, but that seemed pretty far-fetched. Surely if she'd been involved with witness protection, they would have provided better housing, and she wouldn't have gotten involved with a crook like Hank Weller.

"I'm really sorry, Kate." Sincere concern showed in her eyes. "Oh, I almost forgot. There was a small article in the

Tennessean this morning that mentioned that Glynis Maddock was officially identified as the victim of a fatal accident a couple of months ago. Didn't say much except that she and Hank had been living in Copper Mill."

Reaching across her desk, Livvy slipped the Nashville newspaper out from under the *Chronicle*. "It's in the local section under police activity. You're welcome to take that with you if you'd like."

Taking the paper, Kate was thankful for the library's vast subscription to newspapers and for Livvy's devotion to reading them. However, she was also concerned that anyone seeing the article would now have a trail to follow. She decided she'd study the paper at home later. She thanked Livvy for her help and left the library.

The rain that had threatened earlier had started, big drops splashing on the sidewalk. She made a dash to her car. In the distance, she heard the rumble of thunder. The lantern streetlights had come on in a futile battle to keep the darkening gloom away.

She groaned, realizing that she still had to stop at the Mercantile for milk and bread. Three growing children went through staples in a hurry.

She drove the short distance to the store and parked in front. The bright overhead lights inside the Mercantile contrasted with the early dusk settling over the town.

She grabbed a cart and she pushed it to the back of the store where the dairy products were displayed. She noted few shoppers in the store.

"Hey, Kate." Sam Gorman looked up from restocking

shelves with cottage cheese and yogurt to greet her. He wore khaki pants and a white shirt with the cuffs rolled up to his elbows. "You're shopping late today."

"Since the Maddock children moved in with us, I can't keep up with the milk and bread they consume." She pulled two gallons of milk from the refrigerator and put them in her cart.

"Speaking of the Maddock family, a couple of guys were asking about them earlier this afternoon."

A frisson of alarm sparked in Kate's mind. "What guys?"

Sam put the last of the cottage cheese on the shelf. "I didn't get their names. Not from around here, that's for sure. Said they were friends of Glynis from Knoxville."

Friends? Or robbers looking for a stash of diamonds? "What did these men look like?"

Sam lowered his brows. "One guy, the talker, had a husky build, dark hair, and a beard that looked a week old. The other fellow didn't say much. Taller and lankier than the first, narrow face with a beaklike nose. They seemed nice enough." He set the empty carton aside. "Is something wrong?"

"I don't know." Sam's description of the man with the husky build and whiskers could easily fit Perry Weller. "What did you tell them?"

"I told them the Maddocks lived out Smoky Mountain Hollow way. I hope I didn't get Glynis in trouble or anything. They acted a little odd, but I figured no harm done if they were friends of hers."

Briefly she told Sam about Glynis' death and her involvement with a diamond thief.

"Whoa! That's heavy stuff," he said.

"I know. Do me a favor. If they come back, see if you can find out who they are. And don't mention we've got the children at our house."

He frowned and looked worried. "Whatever you say. I hope I didn't stick my foot in it."

The overhead lights flickered, followed by a crack of thunder rumbling across the sky.

He glanced up at the ceiling. "Looks like we may lose power. If the cash registers go down before you check out, you can square your bill with me later."

Kate nodded. The sooner she could get out of here, the better. Because Kate urgently wanted to get to the Maddock trailer and find out who those two men were. *If* they were still around.

Chapter Fourteen

Rain and wind battered the Honda as Kate drove out of town. The windshield wipers battled to keep up with the onslaught. Lightning cracked across the darkening sky. Even at slow speed, Kate's car created a squirrel's tail of water spraying up behind it.

Few other vehicles had ventured out in the torrent. The empty road to Smoky Mountain Hollow loomed ahead like a fast-flowing river of black water. Streetlights were few and far between.

Shortly before she reached the turnoff to the Maddock trailer, a van lurched out onto the road, its headlights on high beam. Kate squinted as the van approached, the lights temporarily blinding her. She barely got a glimpse of the light-colored van just before the vehicle's wake rocked her car. She had to fight to keep the Honda on the road and away from the rain-swollen ditch that drained the water toward Copper Mill Creek.

Peering through the windshield, she spotted the Maddock mailbox alongside the road and the break in the trees that led to the trailer. She turned right and felt her tires leave the asphalt pavement, crunching onto gravel and splashing into potholes.

Her headlights picked up the shadowed silhouette of the trailer. No lights were on inside, no vehicle parked nearby. She pulled up in front of the trailer as close as she could. Rain poured off the trailer roof at the corners in two matching cascades.

Leaving the headlights on, she found the flashlight in the glove box and got out of the car. Maybe she was worried for nothing. Maybe the men who questioned Sam were indeed friends of Glynis, not diamond thieves. But that was hard to believe.

Flashlight in hand, she hurried up to the porch in the drenching rain. She halted briefly at the door. Took a deep breath. And turned the knob. The door swung open, the hinges objecting with a shrill creak.

"Hello . . . ," she called into the dark interior, wondering if she had made a mistake by not calling the police.

Another lightning bolt split the sky and lit up the living room. Kate got a quick view of a mess in the room, and then it was dark again.

Her mouth went dry as she found the light switch and flicked it on. Nothing happened. Hoping the problem was simply a burned-out lightbulb, not a power failure, she made her way across the room to the table lamp by the couch. She moved with care to avoid a cushion that had been thrown to the floor and an overturned coffee table.

She heard the steady splat of water dripping somewhere inside the trailer, as relentless as a beating heart but more ominous.

She turned the knob on the table lamp. A dim circle of light revealed a couch ripped from end to end, the stuffing strewn on the floor. The cushions too, tossed aside, leaked their innards from repeated slashing wounds.

"Dear heavens!" she gasped. An upholstered rocking chair had been torn apart down to its wooden frame. The TV lay facedown in its broken remains.

Gingerly she stepped through the debris, turning lights on as she went. Every cupboard in the kitchen had been emptied, the contents left on the floor, broken and useless. The refrigerator stood open, cleaned out as well.

The bedrooms were the same. Mattresses ripped apart, drawers emptied and turned upside down.

No friends of Glynis had committed this atrocity. No ordinary vandals either.

Thieves in search of diamonds were the culprits. And from the way they'd ransacked the place, she didn't think they'd found what they'd come after.

She needed to call the police. These thieves were more dangerous than she had realized. Thank heavens the children weren't still living there.

Hurrying through the rain, she got into her car and found her cell phone in her purse. Punching in the number of the deputy's office, she reached Skip Spencer. He promised to come right out.

Shivering, Kate waited in the car. Her breath steamed the car windows. Her nerves burned with adrenaline.

Would the culprits return? If they hadn't found the diamonds, would they give up?

She bowed her head and spent several moments in silent prayer for the children's safety—and her own.

Finally, headlights flashed across her car, and Skip's SUV pulled up beside her. Her relief did little to slow her heartbeat.

Wearing a yellow slicker, Skip climbed out of his vehicle with his gun drawn and flashed a light through her windshield.

"Missus Hanlon? That you in there?"

She rolled down her window. "Yes, it's me, Skip."

"Stay where you are, ma'am. I'll check out the trailer. There could still be somebody—"

"There's no one there now." She raised the window and opened her door. "The place has been ransacked."

"Well, let me double-check. I'll call the sheriff just as soon as I reconnoiter."

He marched up to the uneven porch and nearly lost his footing on the second step, barely saving himself by grabbing the handrailing.

Kate followed him up the rickety steps and inside the trailer.

"Oh, wow," he said when he got a look at the mess in the living room. "It's those vandals again. They're escalating. Sheriff's gonna be real upset about—"

"This wasn't done by vandals. It was a pair of thieves looking for diamonds."

Skip looked at her blankly. "I don't think anybody living in this dump would have any diamonds."

"No, you don't understand." Kate tried to explain about Hank Weller and the diamond thieves, but Skip appeared fixated on the idea that the same vandals who'd gone Dumpster diving behind the Mercantile had broken into the Maddock trailer.

"I'll mention the diamond business to Sheriff Roberts," Skip agreed.

"Thanks, Skip." Kate began to wander through the trailer again. She searched for anything else that might be of value, or at least sentimental value, and found little worth recovering.

"This is a crime scene, Missus Hanlon. I have to tape it off." He gestured for her to leave. "I've got some yellow tape in the truck. Best you go home now. The sheriff will take a look in the morning."

Close to acquiescing, a frightening thought occurred to Kate. She hurried into the kitchen where she'd left Glynis a note by the phone so the woman could locate her children if she came home.

To Kate's dismay, the note was no longer beside the phone. She searched the floor. Tried to look behind the counter, but there was no room for anything to have slipped behind the built-in cabinets.

The terrifying realization struck her like a lightning bolt. Her name and phone number had been on that note. It would take little to discover where she lived. And the children.

Perry Weller and his partner knew where to look next for the diamonds.

Chapter Fifteen

Kate hurried home through the heavy rain that continued to fall. She picked up the bag of groceries she'd bought at the Mercantile and went inside, going directly to the kitchen.

Seeing the children already at the dinner table gave her a sense of relief, both because they were safe and because they'd gone ahead with supper. Paul had made them hamburgers, frozen french fries, and a tossed salad.

"We were beginning to worry about you." Paul had changed from his suit into khaki pants and a casual, long-sleeved shirt she'd bought him for his last birthday.

"Sorry I'm so late." She set the groceries on the counter. Her discoveries at the trailer had badly shaken her, and her hands trembled.

"Pastor Paul said he'd help me with my kite after dinner," Beck said, smears of ketchup on both of his cheeks. "I don't have any homework tonight."

"Because we didn't go to school," Gwen pointed out.

"We'll have double homework tomorrow," Megan warned.

The boy scrunched up his nose in distaste. With a determined thrust, he dipped a french fry into a dollop of ketchup on his plate and stuck it in his mouth. It remained obvious that he wasn't keen on the idea of homework.

"Do you think you'll be ready to go to school tomorrow?" Kate asked Megan.

"Might as well," Megan responded with a shrug. "Nothing's going to change by staying home."

"I could stay home tomorrow," Beck volunteered.

Kate wished they'd all stay home, where she could keep them close to her.

KATE WAITED UNTIL AFTER THE CHILDREN were in bed to tell Paul about the ransacked trailer.

They'd just sat down together in the living room when the phone rang. Paul went to answer it in the bedroom. One of the disadvantages of being a pastor was that members of the congregation were likely to call anytime, day or night.

A few minutes later, he returned, grinning, and sat down beside her. "That was Skip. We're on for tomorrow night."

"On for what?"

"A stakeout behind the Mercantile, if the weather clears. We're going to catch those kids who've been messing with Sam's Dumpster and breaking into the ice-cream shop and taking a joyride on the electric cart at the Hamilton Springs Hotel."

"Paul, I'm not sure teenagers are doing all that damage."

"Who else? It's not like Copper Mill has a big homeless population."

"Thankfully, you're right about that." Though Megan had probably come close enough to hunger that she might have been tempted to dig discarded food out of the Dumpster to feed her brother and sister. But since they'd been staying at the parsonage—and under Kate's watchful eye—they couldn't have been the culprits.

"Did you notice the deep scratches on Sam's Dumpster?" she asked.

"Actually, I haven't had a chance to take a look at the Dumpster. Why?"

"I saw the same kind of scratches on the maintenance cart at the hotel. I don't think a teenager would or could have done that kind of damage. Plus, I understand that the back door of Emma's Ice Cream Shop was completely knocked off its hinges."

"The cart was run into a tree. That's how it got damaged. As for Sam's Dumpster, you've seen those trash pickup trucks. They fling Dumpsters twenty feet up in the air, then bash 'em around a few times before they put them back on the ground. I imagine every Dumpster in town is all dented and banged up and has been for years. As for the ice-cream shop, anybody can remove a simple wooden door with a crowbar. What are you getting at anyway, Katie?"

Paul could be very persuasive. That was part of what made him a good minister. Even so, Kate thought he was wrong this time. The damage she'd seen had to have been done by something stronger than a couple of adolescents out on the town.

"Paul, I think an animal is causing all that mischief in town and at the hotel. A large animal, maybe a bear."

He laughed. "Come on, Katie. We don't get bears in town. Why would one wander out of the hills when it has everything it needs right there?"

"Maybe the bear is hungry or injured and can't forage for himself."

"I think you're wrong, honey. Completely off track." His mocking smile brought a teasing glint to his blue eyes that annoyed Kate.

"Maybe," she said sternly. "But I'm asking you and your friends to be extra cautious anyway. None of you are a match for a hungry brown bear. Besides"—she made one last effort to stop the men from doing something foolish—"tomorrow night is choir practice. Sam's the director. He needs to be there."

"Oh, I forgot to tell you. Sam wanted me to tell you he's canceling choir practice this week, so all three of us are good to go."

Kate groaned out loud.

Chapter Sixteen

Kate drove the children to school the next morning and waited until she was sure they were safely inside. The thought that Perry Weller and his buddy might be lurking around had kept her awake half the night.

Hoping to catch the sheriff at the Maddock's trailer, she drove out Smoky Mountain Hollow Road again. The storm had passed through the valley during the night, washing the trees clean and leaving a few puffy white clouds in the sky. Newly grown pine needles shimmered lime green against the blue and white backdrop.

As she turned off the road, she realized that Skip had wrapped crime-scene tape around the trailer porch like he was wrapping a boxer's hands before a big fight, looping the yellow tape over and over again.

She pulled up next to Sheriff Roberts' black-and-white patrol car and stopped. As she got out of the Honda, the sheriff appeared at the trailer door.

A man in his late forties, Alan Roberts had a waistline that suggested he'd consumed too much country cooking.

As Kate approached, he touched the brim of his hat in greeting. "Mornin', Kate."

"Good morning, Sheriff. Looks like you'll have to double the county budget for crime-scene tape next year."

He eyed the yellow tape strung around the rickety porch and chuckled. "Looks like I'll have to start rationing Skip, that's for sure."

She ducked under the tape and walked up the steps.

"You're the one who discovered the vandalism, right?" the sheriff asked.

"Actually, Sheriff, I don't think vandals ransacked the place. I'm quite sure the culprits were a pair of diamond thieves looking for loot they think their partner stashed here."

As she explained what she knew and how she'd become involved with the children, Roberts' bushy eyebrows rose. Finally he dug a frayed notepad out of his pocket and wrote down the criminals' names.

"Were they here last night when you arrived?" he asked.

"No. They'd gone by then." For which Kate was grateful.

"Any idea what kind of vehicle they were driving?"

She started to shake her head, then stopped. "I did see a light-colored van on the road last night. It was raining so hard that I didn't get a close look, but I think it was either white or cream-colored. I don't know for sure, but they may have come out onto the main road from here."

"Any identifying markings on the sides of the van that you could see?"

"It was too dark, and the rain was so heavy, I just tried to stay out of the ditch when the van passed."

"*Hunh*," he mumbled and jotted down another note. "It sure was a gullywasher, I'll say that. Any chance you got a look at who was driving the van?"

"I'm afraid not."

"I'll get out an APB on these two characters and the van. You figure they're still around here someplace?"

"I'm reasonably sure they didn't find the diamonds or they wouldn't have ransacked the whole place. I'm afraid they'll go after the Maddock children next, thinking the kids may know where the diamonds are hidden."

Roberts scratched his head, then resettled his hat in place. "Seems odd that Hank Weller would go off to Nashville and leave the diamonds behind."

"Unless he was expecting to come back and had hidden them exceptionally well." She glanced toward the woods behind the trailer, wondering if the diamonds could be buried there and how anyone would find them if they were.

"The only unusual thing highway patrol found in Hank's car was a bag of Becker's marbles. He's Glynis' nine-year-old son."

"*Hunh*," he commented again.

"I'm wondering what to do with the trailer and the children's personal effects."

"I checked the county property records before I came out here this morning. This trailer belongs to some guy in Chattanooga. I'm guessing Glynis or Hank rented the trailer from him, probably furnished. I'll give him a call when I get back to the office."

"Then it's only the personal effects I have to worry about. And the children's safety."

"I'd say that's about it."

Kate thought about something else that had been bothering her: the reason the children wanted to steer clear of the police.

"Have you found any reason they would be afraid to trust the neighbors?"

"I took a walk around the property when I first arrived this morning. Thought there might be a still operating back in the woods."

"Did you find anything?"

"Not on this property. But I'd say a neighbor a couple of lots down the road is cookin' up some good ol' white lightning. I plan to let the feds know about that, although it's pretty common in the hollows. It won't surprise them any."

Kate was relieved to think the neighbors' activities might explain why the children had been warned to stay clear of both the people living nearby and the police.

As KATE WAITED to pick up the children from school that afternoon, she kept an eye out for a white or beige van. She drummed her fingers on the steering wheel. She hated that they might be the target of two violent criminals.

Finally the three children piled into her car.

"How'd the day go?" Kate asked.

"Beck got in trouble and had to go to the principal's office," Gwen announced, almost gleefully.

Kate turned sideways so she could see Beck. "What happened?"

"Billy Gotshaw called me a stupid orphan, and I hit him."

Kate winced. What a cruel thing for a child to say.

Megan turned on her brother. "We're *not* orphans! Pa's still alive."

His lip quivering, Beck asked, "So where is he?"

I wish I knew, Kate thought. "Was Mrs. Walner upset with you?"

"Nuh-uh. She gave me a sucker and said she understood."

Kate wasn't sure that was the best reaction to the boy's violent outburst but decided to shelve any lectures for now.

Once home, the somber children settled down with their homework and an afternoon snack at the kitchen table. With Paul in town on business, Kate tried to help Beck with his reading. He struggled manfully to get through the assignment, but he was clearly frustrated by the effort.

When the doorbell rang, Beck hopped up to see who was there.

Kate held him back. "You stay put. I'll take care of whoever's at the door." She'd been reluctant to tell the children that they might be in danger. They'd already had too much to handle in their young lives. But she didn't want them to inadvertently open the door to someone who might want to harm them.

She looked through the peephole. The moment Kate opened the door, Renee blew right past her, Kisses in tow.

"How are the little darlings today?" Without stopping for an answer, Renee barreled her way to the kitchen. "There you are, sweet things. Little Umpkins has been worried about you all day." She hugged each child and gave them air kisses.

"We're fine, Miz Lambert," Megan said.

Renee fluttered her long, artificial fingernails in the air. "Oh, do call me something besides Mrs. Lambert. It makes me feel ancient, and of course, I'm not that old."

Perplexed, the children stared at her wide-eyed.

With an effort, Kate held her tongue. She knew Renee had already seen her seventieth birthday.

"You may call me Auntie Renee. How's that?" Renee beamed.

Megan shrugged. "Fine, I guess."

Kisses popped his head out of the tote. Gwen rewarded him with a scratch under his chin.

"Well, now, I see you're doing your homework." Renee flitted from one child to the next. "You know, I was once a very good student. If you need any help with any little thing, you just ask."

"You smell funny," Beck said.

"Why, young man, I'll have you know what you're smelling is the finest fragrance in the world, Estée Lauder's Youth Dew."

Beck didn't look convinced, and Kate could see that Megan was doing her best not to laugh out loud.

"Why don't I fix us some tea while the children are working?" Kate offered.

"Perfect. I can sit right here at the table where I'll be handy if they have any questions."

Kate set the kettle on the stove to heat and got down two of her nicest teacups and a matching pot.

At the table, Renee whispered to Beck, who was working on some math problems, "Use your fingers to count. I always do."

Kate smothered a smile.

She'd managed to get two cups of tea poured when the doorbell rang again. Raising her hand, she let everyone know she'd take care of the caller, whoever it was.

Through the peephole, she saw a tall, angular woman with

graying hair and a dour expression, not the pair of criminals she feared might appear at any moment.

She opened the door partway.

"Mrs. Hanlon?" Kate acknowledged that she was, and the woman continued. "I am Valerie Hyland with the Department of Children's Services. I understand you are caring for three children whose mother has recently passed."

Kate threw an anxious glance over her shoulder toward the dining room, then turned back to her caller. "Do you have some identification, Ms. Hyland?"

The woman looked put out that Kate had asked for her ID. From her shoulder bag, she produced an official-looking badge and held it out for Kate to examine.

"How did you hear about the children?" Kate asked.

"We have a close working relationship with the schools, Mrs. Hanlon. The best interests of the children are our mutual priority. If I might come in . . ."

Apparently Arletta Walner had blown the whistle on Kate and the kids, all with good intentions, Kate was sure. Nonetheless, she didn't appreciate a social worker showing up at her door unannounced, but she couldn't think of any reason to keep the woman out.

She opened the door the rest of the way.

"You do understand, Ms. Hyland, that the news of their mother's death has been very difficult for the children. I'd appreciate it if you didn't upset them any further."

"Of course." Dressed in a plain navy blue suit and white blouse, the social worker stood in the middle of the living room looking around. "You have an unusually large room here, Mrs. Hanlon."

"My husband's the pastor of Faith Briar Church. Sometimes we have meetings of the congregation here at the parsonage."

"I see." She seemed unimpressed. "I'd like to see where the children sleep, if I may."

Kate got a bad feeling. "Why?"

"Mrs. Hanlon, the state sets very high standards when it comes to nonfamily members acting in a custodial role for minor children. While you're not officially approved as foster parents, the state may be able to show some flexibility if . . . and I repeat *if* the accommodations you provide are considered adequate and I judge that you and your husband are suitable."

"I assure you, Ms. Hyland, my husband and I raised three children of our own, all of whom are quite successful adults. We are up to the task."

The social worker thrust out her pointed chin. "That's not the point. If you will be so kind as to show me where the children sleep."

Renee and the children had stopped what they'd been doing and were watching Kate with concern, Gwen and Beck huddled beside their big sister. Kate didn't want to alarm them if she could avoid it.

"Very well." She marched to Paul's study and stood by the doorway, gratified to see the foldout bed made up and no clothes scattered about. "Megan and her sister sleep here."

"Your husband's office?"

"We refer to it as his study, which doubles as a guest room. The bed's quite comfortable, I assure you. My children and their spouses sleep in it when they visit."

"I see. And young Becker? Where does he sleep?"

"We've put up a privacy screen for him so he has his own

little area." Annoyed that the social worker hadn't even asked to meet the children, much less spend some time getting to know them, Kate gestured toward the corner of the living room that they'd arranged for Beck.

"Oh, no no no." Ms. Hyland sternly shook her head. "Simply not suitable. Not at all."

"Beck's been quite comfortable here. Granted, he sleeps on an air mattress, but my grandchildren have never minded that. It's like camping out."

"The state's rules are very clear. Children may share a bedroom if they are of the same sex, but they are not allowed to sleep in a public area such as this."

Renee joined Kate. "What's going on?"

"Ms. Hyland's a social worker. She's checking up on the children. This is my friend and a member of our congregation, Renee Lambert," she said by way of introduction.

"They're lovely children," Renee said. "Dear little things. It's all so sad, them losing their mother."

"Yes, of course. But I am charged with making sure that the children are properly housed and well supervised. Since there is no father in the picture—"

"I'm attempting to locate him," Kate interjected.

"—and no other known relatives, I am obligated to act on their behalf. If my home study reveals an unsuitable arrangement, then I will be forced—"

"Are you saying you're going to remove these kids from my house?" Kate asked, aghast at the possibility. "They're only here temporarily, until I can locate their father and make some other arrangement. They've just lost their mother and their home. You can't mean to uproot them again so soon."

"The Hanlons are wonderful people," Renee said, looking at the woman so severely that a thick vein popped out on her forehead. "I can't imagine a better family for these children at this difficult time in their lives."

The social worker rose up to her full five-feet-ten inches. "Becker cannot sleep in the living room. It's as simple as that."

It was all Kate could do to hold her temper in check. "Then I'll put him somewhere else. He'll be fine."

"Where?"

Kate tried to think. She hadn't wanted to put Beck in her studio because of all the glass and cutting tools. It wouldn't be safe.

"I'll clean out my studio and move his bed in there."

Looking down her nose at Kate, Ms. Hyland said, "I don't believe I care for your attitude, Mrs. Hanlon. I am under no obligation to keep the children in these unacceptable conditions."

Kate wanted to roll her eyes but didn't dare.

"I believe the solution to this situation is quite simple." Renee waggled her fingers in the air. "I have a lovely home here in town with ample bedrooms. We can move the children to my house for as long as is necessary."

"What about—" Kate almost asked how Renee's mother would feel about that but clamped her mouth shut instead. In some ways, it might be safer for the children to stay with Renee. Perry Weller and his buddy wouldn't know where to find them.

"They'll still be able to visit the Hanlons," Renee continued. "Whom they've become very fond of. And I do believe you'll find the accommodations I can provide for the children quite adequate."

Ms. Hyland frowned. "Do you know these children well?"

"They call me Auntie Renee," she said smugly. "They adore me."

The social worker hesitated. "I don't mean to be indelicate, but . . ." she coughed. "These are three active children . . ."

"*Really!* There's no need to be insulting." Renee lifted her head, setting her bleached-blonde hair into motion. "I don't consider thirty-nine to be old."

Valerie Hyland didn't appear convinced that Renee hadn't yet reached her fortieth birthday. Kate didn't think this was the time to argue about it, however.

Reluctantly, Ms. Hyland agreed to allow the children to stay with the Hanlons for one more night. She explained that she would complete a home study the following morning to see if Renee could provide a suitable foster-care situation for the children. Kate was instructed to have the kids' belongings packed and ready to go in any event. Beck, at least, could not remain in the Hanlon household under the current arrangement, and his sisters refused to let him go without them.

The Maddock siblings would *not* be separated.

By the time the social worker left, Kate was exhausted and nearly in tears, the children were distraught, and Renee had assumed the role of soothing friend and loving aunt.

The Lord works in mysterious ways, Kate mused.

Chapter Seventeen

After a dinner that starred three anxious children and a wife embattled by Children's Services, Paul went into the bedroom to change into jeans and a navy blue slip-over sweater. He wanted to blend into the shadows behind the Mercantile while he, Sam, and Skip waited to trap the vandals.

As upset as Kate was about the social worker's decision to move the children, she understood they might be safer elsewhere until the diamond thieves were caught, or until their father was found and other arrangements for their care could be made.

He smoothed his rapidly graying hair and picked out a dark cap to wear, then studied his reflection in the mirror. Adding camouflage makeup seemed a little over the top, just as Skip's grand military-style plan had been.

He found Kate and Megan in the kitchen cleaning up the dinner dishes.

"I'll be on my way now . . ." He paused. "If you and the kids think you'll be okay on your own."

"We're all right." Kate set aside the dish she'd been drying. A slight frown etched itself into her forehead. "I made you a thermos of coffee to take along. You'll need a jacket too. It'll get cold sitting out there all night."

"We'll be fine, but the coffee's a good idea. Thanks."

"Why don't you take one of our camp stools so you'll have somewhere to sit?"

He tucked a few strands of Kate's strawberry-blonde hair behind her ear. "Honey, we'll be fine. We'll catch the kids who've been vandalizing the town, scare the snot out of them, and I'll be back home in no time."

"Well, just in case the 'kids' are much bigger than you expect, maybe you should take a baseball bat with you," she said.

"I promise, if we spot a bear behind the Mercantile, I'll be the first one out of there and running for the hills."

"But can you run faster than a wild animal?"

Paul hoped he'd never have to learn the answer to that question.

He kissed Kate and told the children good night. He wasn't sure what time he'd get home.

As he drove to town in his pickup, and darkness began to fall across the countryside, he felt a lightness of spirit. In its own small way, this was going to be an adventure.

He parked the truck at the end of the alley where an intruder wouldn't notice it. Grabbing the thermos and a flash-light, he strolled toward the back of the Mercantile, the soles of his shoes scraping on the gritty asphalt. Every hundred feet or so, a dim security light created an orange glow that did little to illuminate the alley.

The buildings backing onto the alley filtered the night sounds of town. A passing car on Main Street hummed along the road. A TV played softly in a nearby apartment, but Paul couldn't make out the words. In the distance, a sleepless rooster announced the coming of dawn hours too soon.

"Paul!" Skip's whispered call came out of the darkness. "We're over here."

He angled in that direction. "Kate made us coffee."

"Great!" Sam said. "Make yourself at home."

Using empty wooden crates, Sam and Skip had created something that resembled a duck blind, where they could see the Mercantile's Dumpster and yet not be seen by passersby. The two of them sat deep in the shadows where Paul could barely make them out.

"It's dark tonight," Paul said. "Maybe we should've waited for a full moon."

"I'm tired of sweeping up the mess those vandals leave behind." Sam guided Paul to an upended crate. "Pull up a chair and sit yourself down."

Gingerly, Paul perched on the edge of the crate. Kate was right. He should have brought along a camp stool.

"Don't you have some folding camp chairs in stock, Sam?" he asked. "This is going to get uncomfortable after a few hours."

"Stakeouts are a tough assignment," Skip pointed out.

Paul eyed the Dumpster across the alley. The faint scent of spoiled meat drifted in the air. "You bait the Dumpster, Sam? It smells pretty ripe."

"Trash pickup is tomorrow. That's why we're here tonight. The other two times the vandals hit me, the Dumpster was nearly full. That's when they can make the biggest mess. I figure their folks aren't home at night or something, so the kids are free to get into some mischief."

"That's a reasonable theory."

"Shh, you two," Skip ordered. "No talking. You'll spook our unsubs."

"Unsubs?" Paul questioned.

"Unknown subjects," Skip explained with a superior inflection in his voice.

Adjusting his position, Paul leaned back against the block wall fence that ran between the alley and older homes that faced Ashland Street. A chair would have been much more comfortable than one of these wobbly crates with splinters that poked through his jeans.

Suddenly Skip sat up. "Listen! I hear something."

Paul detected the faint shuffle of shoes on the asphalt. The sound came closer. *Crunch, crunch. Crunch, crunch.*

"Let 'em get real close," Skip ordered in a hoarse whisper, "then we'll jump 'em."

As the footsteps came closer, Paul's heart rate picked up and his breathing grew shallow. Could it really be that easy? They'd been there no more than a half hour—

A new sound reached Paul. A low-throated growl.

"Hold it right where you are!" Skip jumped up from his hiding place and switched on his heavy-duty flashlight. The beam sliced through the night and found a target Paul recognized.

"Help! Police!" Orson Ulrich screamed.

His Doberman lunged at Skip at the end of his leash and bared his teeth.

Skip fell backward over a crate in his effort to get away. "I am the police, Orson. Call off your dog. Call him off now!"

Sam tried to pull Skip away from the dog, who had his teeth firmly latched onto Skip's pant leg.

"Sunshine, let go of him," Orson ordered. "What in tarnation are you doin' out here in the middle of the night?" The eighty-year-old yanked on the dog's leash again. "You heard me. Leave him alone. Come!"

"The question is, what are you doing here, Mr. Ulrich?" Skip asked.

Paul didn't think the old man could be the vandal they were looking for, but he supposed that stranger things had happened.

Orson managed to regain control of his dog. "What do you think I'm doin'? I'm walkin' my dog, that's what."

Sam stepped forward, apologetic. He explained about the vandals.

"You fool people pull a stunt like this again, and I'm reporting you to the sheriff. Terrorizing people is against the law, you know." He yanked on the leash again. "Come on, Sunshine. Let's get out of here."

Still muttering under his breath, Orson marched back the way he had come.

Skip exhaled loudly. "That didn't go so well."

"Did the dog hurt you?" Paul asked.

"Naw, but I'm gonna need a new pair of pants." The deputy flicked his hand across the ripped material where the dog had latched on to him.

The team regrouped and settled back down on their crates. Cool air crept under Paul's jacket. He zipped it up and stuck his hands in his pockets. Without a full moon to steal the light from the stars, the heavens were filled with a million twinkling pinpricks. The North Star glowed brightly, leading the way to the Big Dipper.

In the beginning God created the heavens and the earth.

As Paul pondered the enormity of that truth, an unfamiliar sound drew his attention. For a moment he couldn't identify what it was or who was making it. Then he realized it was Skip snoring.

"Sam? You awake?" Paul whispered.

"I'm here."

"Sounds like Skip just flunked Stakeout 101."

Sam chuckled as they listened to Skip's rhythmic intake of air.

Almost an hour later, Paul spotted movement near the Dumpster. He nudged Skip and strained to get a clearer view of whoever was approaching.

Skip woke with a snort. "Wha—"

"Shh, we've got somebody."

Sam got to his feet, staring ahead. Paul looked in the direction of Sam's gaze, stunned by the sight.

"Well, don't that beat all," Sam said. "A bear cub's been raiding my Dumpster."

The little brown bear stood on his back feet pushing at the heavy lid, trying to gain access to the tempting smells inside. Either he wasn't strong enough to do the job or didn't have the right leverage.

"I'm gonna run that critter off." Sam picked up a stick and a metal trash-can lid he'd brought along to frighten teenage hooligans.

Paul jumped to his feet. "Wait, Sam!"

Banging the stick on the lid like a snare drum, Sam strolled toward the cub. "Get on outta here, buddy!"

"Be careful," Skip said.

"Sam, the cub's mother could be—"

Before Paul could finish his warning, a big lumbering figure came into view, loping unevenly from out of the shadows. She gave a cry that sent the cub scampering to safety, then turned on Sam. She rose up on her back legs and roared. One of her paws appeared injured.

"Sam! Get out of there!" Paul said.

Sam remained frozen in place. So did Skip.

"Do something, Skip." Paul grabbed a crate and waved it in the air to make himself appear as large as he could to the bear. He scooted out of the blind to help his friend. "Get outta here, bear! Go on! You've got no business here."

Paul snared Sam's arm and started walking backward away from the bear. The bear dropped to all fours but didn't give ground.

A shot rang out and banged harmlessly into the Dumpster. The bear turned her attention toward Skip.

"Don't shoot her, Skip. Just walk away slowly." Paul kept his eye on the big animal.

Skip broke into a run, going in the same direction the cub had fled.

"No, Skip, don't—"

Mama bear took off after Skip at a lope that closed the distance fast.

"Aw, Skip—" Paul forced Sam into a run to get to his truck. "We've gotta help him."

Finally coming out of his frozen stupor, Sam got to the

truck and climbed into the passenger side. Paul got behind the wheel, switched on the ignition, and turned the headlights to high beam. He roared down the alley after Skip and the bear.

Skip had made it safely to his SUV, but so had the bear. She was up on her hind feet, rocking the deputy's vehicle for all she was worth.

Paul laid on his truck horn, trying to frighten her off. She gave the SUV one more shake for good measure, then dropped to all fours and lumbered off into the darkness.

Sam blew out a long breath. "Guess I was wrong about the vandals being teenagers."

"Yep. We can both say that."

SHORTLY AFTER MIDNIGHT, Kate heard Paul's truck arrive home. She'd gone to bed, but she hadn't been able to go to sleep. Even if Paul hadn't gone out, she was too upset about the children and what would become of them to sleep anyway.

Her head on the pillow, she waited for him in the bedroom.

He opened the door quietly and slipped into the room.

"How'd it go?" she asked.

"I thought you'd be asleep. I was trying not to wake you."

She switched on the light beside the bed. "I always waited up for the children when they were out late. It seems only fair I wait up for you too."

"You were worried, weren't you?" He gave her a wry smile before pulling his sweater off over his head.

"About you and the children," she said. "Did you catch the vandals?"

"In a manner of speaking." He sat down on the edge of the bed and started to take off his shoes.

Kate suspected there was a reason he didn't want to talk about what happened. "I was right, wasn't I?"

"Yes, Katie, you were right. The biggest mama bear you ever saw, and her cub. Skip's going to call the fish-and-wildlife authorities in the morning. It looked like the bear had been injured, maybe in an illegal bear trap, which is why she couldn't forage for herself and her cub up in the hills where they belong. She was looking for easy pickings in town." He glanced over at her with another wry smile. "You'd think after all these years, I'd learn to listen to you."

She sat up in bed. "Was anyone hurt?"

"Skip got the worst of it. His pants were ripped by a dog."

"A dog?"

"Orson Ulrich was walking his Doberman, who didn't take kindly to us surprising them in the alley."

Kate suppressed a smile.

"The bear gave Skip's SUV a working over too. It's going to need a few dents taken out and a new paint job. Same kind of scratches you pointed out on the hotel's electric cart. Sheriff Roberts isn't likely to take kindly to having to fix the SUV either."

"Sounds like your evening was a mixed success."

"To add insult to my stupidity, in all the excitement, I forgot to bring the thermos home. I'll get it tomorrow."

When he slid into bed beside Kate, he pulled her into his arms. "Next time I come up with some cockamamy scheme, remind me what a smart woman I married."

"I'd be happy to, sweetie." She smiled to herself and kissed her husband good night.

Chapter Eighteen

Thursday morning was bittersweet for Kate. Kate had helped the children pack their scant belongings in a couple of suitcases she had stored in the garage last night. The suitcases were lined up now by the garage door, along with Megan's box of cornhusks and supplies for her dolls. The kids decided to leave the kite project with the Hanlons in the hope that Paul could help them finish the job before Old Timer's Day the following week.

Megan stood by the kitchen window looking out at the garden. "We haven't finished planting the garden yet."

"When things settle down, you can come back and help me finish." Kate slid her arm around Megan's waist. "You'll be all right with Renee, won't you?"

She shrugged. "Sure. I'll watch after Gwen and Beck like I always do."

Tears stung Kate's eyes, and she desperately tried to hold them back. "You'll have to be careful, Megan. Hank's brother and a friend may be looking for you."

Slanting a look at Kate, Megan frowned. "Would they hurt my brother and sister?"

"I'll be honest with you, honey . . . it's possible. So stay close to Renee's house until the sheriff can track the brother down. No one will know where to find you there." Kate wasn't sure how much to tell Megan about Perry Weller. She didn't want to frighten the girl but felt she had to urge caution. "You'll be fine with Renee."

"And Kisses," Megan said with a halfhearted smile.

Kate wrote her cell-phone number on a piece of paper and handed it to Megan. "If you need anything, anything at all, call me. Promise?"

"Sure." The girl glanced at the number, neatly folded the note, and stuck it in the pocket of her jeans. "We'd better go or we'll be late."

Rounding up the children, Kate drove them to school. She gave each child a big hug and a kiss.

"I'm going to take your things to Renee's house now. She'll pick you up after school. You wait right here in front of the school for her. Okay?"

Acknowledging her instructions, the threesome trudged up the walk to the main entrance, one sibling on each side of Megan.

Kate's throat was thick with grief and worry. It was hard enough as an adult to face the death of a parent. For children with nowhere else to turn, the pain of loss was doubly difficult.

Somehow Kate had to locate their father. He had to know of someone who could help his children.

She drove the short distance to Renee's house, and Renee watched from the porch while Kate made three trips to the car to bring the children's things inside. For the time being, she left them in the entryway.

"Has the social worker been here yet?" Kate asked.

"She was at my door at eight o'clock this morning." Dressed in a pink velour robe, Renee fluttered her fingers toward the kitchen. "Mother and I hadn't had a chance to have our morning tea yet. I made it quite clear to that woman that calling so early in the day was a serious breach of etiquette."

Apparently Renee was unaware of, or preferred to ignore, her own habit of showing up at Kate's door at the crack of dawn.

"Well, keep the children close to home for a few days." Kate explained in some detail about the possible danger the kids faced from Perry Weller and his partner and apologized for not telling Renee about it sooner. "Keep an eye out for a white or cream-colored van too," she warned.

"Don't you worry about a thing, dear. Mother and I will take good care of them. I promise."

She reminded Renee once more that she should pick the children up after school and then headed to the Mercantile to buy some trash bags. She wanted to make one more effort to find some record of Wyn Maddock in Glynis' effects, as well as deal with the mess the diamond thieves had created.

SEVERAL HOURS LATER, Kate had thrown out six big bags of trash, found a few more family snapshots, and uncovered a box filled with old bills and receipts, which she planned to go through later.

When she finally got back home, she fixed herself a chicken salad tossed with diced apple, slivered almonds, and a spicy peanut dressing. She settled down at the dining table to catch up with the news in the *Copper Mill Chronicle*.

To her dismay, the bold headline read ACCIDENT VICTIM'S HOME RANSACKED. A photo of the Maddocks' run-down trailer appeared above the newspaper fold.

She quickly read through the article, which quoted the police report. No doubt Jennifer McCarthy was only doing her job as a reporter and checked police activity daily.

Kate also recalled that Jennifer was in the library on Monday when Kate had learned of Glynis' death, which had apparently alerted the reporter to a possible local story.

Biting her lip, Kate found that Jennifer had done a thorough job of reporting. Perhaps too thorough. She'd indicated Glynis Maddock's three school-age children, previous residents of Knoxville, were staying with a local pastor's family, naming Kate and Paul Hanlon. While their address wasn't given, it wouldn't take a genius to check the telephone book for that information.

Kate didn't know how Jennifer discovered that the children were staying with her and Paul, but any number of people in town knew.

"Oh, Jennifer, you don't know what you've done," she complained out loud. If Perry Weller happened to see the article, it was like waving a red flag in front of his nose.

She shoved her half-eaten chicken salad aside. If Sheriff Roberts' APB didn't result in the arrest of Weller and Smedley soon, it might be safer to move the children to a whole different county or another state.

After washing up her lunch dishes, she retrieved the box

of Glynis' bills and receipts from her car. She'd just started going through them when the phone rang.

She answered in the kitchen. "Hanlon residence."

After a moment, an older female voice said, "You Kate Hanlon or the maid?"

Kate smiled. "I'm Kate Hanlon, and I wish I had a maid. Can I help you?"

"You was up here in Knoxville some time back askin' about Glynis Maddock and left me your number."

Kate's heart nearly leaped out of her chest. The caller had to be the tiny gray-haired woman who lived across from Glynis' old apartment.

"Yes, I'm the one."

"I saw in the newspaper she got herself kilt in a car crash off in Nashville."

"Yes, I was sorry to learn that too. Were you a good friend of Glynis'?"

"Good enough, I guess. Knew the kids too. Minded their manners real good."

The woman seemed eager to talk about Glynis, so Kate didn't interrupt.

"Thing is, I thought them youngsters would like to know she skedaddled out of Copper Mill with that crook Hank Weller 'cuz she knew his brother was comin' after him. She was afraid the brother would hurt her kids if she let Hank stick around any longer."

"How do you know that?" Kate asked carefully.

"'Cuz I called and warned her that Hank's crazy brother was comin' after him. Told her to get outta there."

Suddenly Kate realized Glynis must have been on the phone talking to her former neighbor when she wrote the note Run! Run!! Run!!! She must have been terrified to learn that Hank's brother was after them and knew that she and Hank had to leave town in a hurry.

"Do you think that by leaving Copper Mill, Glynis was trying to protect her children, not desert them?" Glynis must have planned to leave Hank in Nashville and return to her children that same weekend. The poor woman's plan had gone dreadfully awry.

"Mercy me, she wouldn't desert her babies. Loved 'em like there was no tomorrow. Guess now there won't be no tomorrow for her, huh?"

"No, there won't." The knowledge that Glynis had died protecting the children buoyed Kate's spirits. That was something positive the children could cling to. "Did Glynis ever mention to you where her husband, Wyn Maddock, was?"

"Locked up in some prison or other is what she said. But his name's not Maddock. That's her maiden name. She took it back after they locked her man up for running some poor guy down when he was drunk as a skunk, and she divorced him. Thought the kids would do better with her name than his. They was so young when he went to jail, don't think they ever knew they had a different name."

Kate carried the phone to the kitchen table and sat down heavily in a chair. She'd considered the possibility that Glynis had switched back to her maiden name after the divorce, but she'd been stymied when Megan didn't recall the difference.

Which meant it was no surprise she hadn't been able to

locate Wyn Maddock. He didn't exist. Which was also the reason she hadn't been able to locate the children's birth records.

"Do you know what his last name is?"

On the other end of the line, the woman sucked in a breath as though she was smoking. "Don't recall Glynis ever saying."

"Did you ever meet him?"

"Nope. He was long gone by the time she moved in here."

"Where did she live before she moved into that apartment building?"

The woman hacked a deep-throated cough, and it was several seconds before she was able to speak again. "Talked about living in a house before, but I don't know exactly where. The owners of these here apartments might know."

Hope flared in Kate's chest. If she could track Glynis back to a prior address, her husband's name might be on the lease. "Could you give me the owners' names and a phone number so I can talk to them?"

"Don't imagine it'll do Glynis any harm now if you talk to them."

"It might help her children if I can locate their father." If nothing else, he would have a right to some say about where his children should live, which might keep the siblings from being separated.

Kate wrote down the landlord's name and phone number and also got the woman's name and number in case she had more questions later.

Thanking the woman profusely, Kate hung up and imme-diately dialed the landlord.

To her dismay, an answering machine picked up. She left a message.

For the next hour or so, she plowed through the box of Glynis' receipts, looking for any hint of her married name, but had no luck at all.

Frustrated by her lack of progress, she decided to work in her studio. With only slightly more than a week to go until Old Timer's Day, she was well behind in making more stained-glass pieces for Steve to sell. Maybe working on the pieces would do her some good. Often when she was working with stained glass—or baking—and her right brain was fully engaged, it seemed as though her left brain automatically processed whatever problems she faced, and frequently an answer would come to her.

She pulled her stool up to her worktable in the studio and uncovered the sun catcher she'd been working on. The light danced off the golden petals of the sunflower and seemed to warm the verdant green leaves of glass.

She picked up her glass cutter and began to shape bits of bright blue that would fit into the unfinished sky, providing a backdrop for the sunflower.

Time moved like the gentle flow of a river toward the distant sea. The routine of cut, fit, and trim soothed Kate's troubled mind. The work absorbed her attention in a comforting embrace, the silence in the house settling around her like an old friend she hadn't seen in a long time.

Paul's voice calling her startled Kate back to the moment.

"I'm in the studio," she answered, amazed that the sun catcher was nearly complete. One more piece right there, and she was done. She fitted the bit of glass into place.

Paul appeared at the studio door, wearing a tan sport coat and dark brown slacks. "The house sure is quiet without the kids here. Did you get them settled at Renee's?"

She glanced at her watch and discovered it was a little after four o'clock. "She was picking them up from school. I'm sure she would have called if anything had gone wrong."

"You make any progress in locating their father?"

"Yes and no." She told him about the phone call from Glynis' neighbor in Knoxville. "At least now I know I was looking for the wrong name. I've put a call in to the landlord to see if he can find anything in his records about Glynis' married name. He hasn't called back yet."

Rotating her neck and shoulders to ease the strain of sitting hunched over her worktable for so long, Kate stood up. "Guess I should start thinking about what to have for dinner."

"We can go out, if you'd like. I know you're missing the kids."

"It's all right. I can whip up something just for the two of us easily enough."

As she passed him by, he took hold of her, using his thumbs to massage her tense neck and shoulder muscles.

"*Mmm*, that feels good." She sighed with pleasure. Husbands were wonderful creatures to have around.

"Skip tells me the fish-and-wildlife authorities found the trail that the bears have been using to come into town. They've set up a safe trap to catch the mama bear and her cub. They'll treat the mother's injury and transport her and her cub to an unpopulated area higher in the mountains."

"Then the bears will be all right?"

"Should be, as long as they stay away from town."

"I'm glad." She turned and slipped into his arms. "You know, I have a better idea about dinner. Why don't we stop at the Country Diner, pick up a salad or some sandwiches, and have a picnic on the Town Green, just the two of us?"

"Sounds good to me. Let me change clothes, and it's a date. We'll have an early dinner."

She decided to freshen up a bit too.

"Let me call Renee before we go," Kate said. "Make sure she and her mother are handling everything okay."

Paul smiled knowingly. "You miss the children already, don't you?"

"I suppose I do." Picking up the phone on the kitchen counter, she dialed Renee's house.

"We're doing wonderfully well," Renee assured her. "Umpkins is in seventh heaven playing with Gwen and Beck. Megan's working on a charming cornhusk doll at our kitchen table. I may have to buy it myself."

"Did they do their homework?"

"Oh, we'll get to that later. They need a little relaxation first."

"Sounds good. I just wanted to check in before Paul and I go to dinner."

"Go on and have a good time, dear. The children are fine with Mother and me, and Little Umpkins."

After thanking Renee, Kate hung up, then eyed the phone again.

Paul handed Kate her purse. "Ready now, honey?"

"Ready." The landlord probably wouldn't phone after five o'clock anyway, she figured. And if he did, he'd leave a message.

Just as Paul drove his pickup out of the driveway onto the road, an aging green pickup came charging toward them, going far faster than the speed limit. The vehicle swerved around them, and the driver nearly lost control as he careened onto the wrong side of the road and back again, tires squealing and kicking up dust from the shoulder.

"Good grief!" Shaken, Paul slowed and pulled over to the side of the road. "That guy must be crazy or drunk, driving like that."

"Thank the Lord he didn't—" Kate halted midthought. "That's it!"

"What's it?"

"The children told me their father had *killed* someone. But the woman who called today said he'd been driving drunk. He didn't *murder* his victim, not like shooting or stabbing him. He must have been charged with felony vehicular manslaughter. Not homicide."

"Neither choice is a particularly good one."

She turned to face her husband. "But don't you see? I asked Livvy to check for homicide cases around the time the father was arrested. There were no records of any murders committed by a Wyn by any last name. But there was a drunk-driving fatality. We didn't research that because I had the crime all wrong." And the name too.

His brow furrowed. "Are you sure?"

"No, I'm not sure of anything. But it makes so much sense, I have to be on the right track." She dug her cell phone out of her handbag. "I'm going to call Livvy."

She punched in the number and listened to the phone ring. After the fifth ring, the call went to Livvy's answering machine, which meant she'd probably gone home for the day.

Kate groaned, then left a message asking Livvy to call as soon as possible. She snapped her phone closed.

Even if she found the children's father, Kate warned herself, there was no guarantee he would be able or willing to help them. He hadn't had any contact with his children in years.

Chapter Nineteen

The Hanlons' phone rang early the next morning while Kate and Paul were washing up their breakfast dishes. Kate dried her hands and answered the phone.

Livvy greeted her. "Sorry I didn't get back to you last night, Kate. We went to James' baseball game in Pine Ridge. It went into extra innings, so we got home late."

"No problem. Are you at the library now?" Kate slid a pad of paper toward her on the counter and found a pencil.

"Yes. I had some paperwork to finish this morning, so I came in early. What can I do for you?"

"Do you have time to check something for me?"

"Sure. Let me open the search program." In the background, computer keys clicked as Livvy worked. "All right, what do you need?"

"Last Monday when you were looking up homicide reports in Knoxville nine years ago, you came across a drunk-driving incident that caused a fatality. Can you find that report again?"

"No problem."

Kate glanced at Paul, who had finished putting the dishes away and was listening to her conversation. He gave her an encouraging nod.

"I think I've got the one," Livvy said, relaying the date of the incident. "Driver charged with DUI and vehicular manslaughter."

"What's the driver's name?" Kate held her breath.

"Arthur W. Carew Jr., age thirty-nine."

Kate frowned as she wrote the name on the notepad. "Do you suppose the *W* could stand for Wyn?" She knew that people who were named after their parents often used a middle name to avoid confusion.

"I suppose it could," Livvy replied.

"The problem is that Glynis Maddock changed back to her maiden name after she divorced her husband." Making it doubly difficult for Kate to track him down.

"You think that this Carew fellow could be the father of those three Maddock children?"

"Yes, I do. Can I ask another favor of you, Liv?"

"Of course."

"The Tennessee prison system has a prisoner-locating service on their Web site. Your Internet service is way faster than my dial-up. Can you go to that Web site and type in his name? Let's see if he's still a guest of the state."

"Hang on a minute."

Crossing her fingers and holding her breath, Kate waited again.

"Got him! He's an inmate at Turney Center Industrial Prison."

Kate asked Livvy the location of the Turney Center Industrial Prison and wrote down all the information.

"Thank you so much, Liv."

"I just hope this is the man you're looking for."

"So do I."

WITHIN MINUTES, Kate was dressed in a business suit and on the road to the Turney Center Industrial Prison, which was west of Nashville. She hoped to get there before noon, visit Wyn, and be back home by late afternoon with good news— *oh, please!*—for the children.

The interstate took her toward Nashville, around the center of the city, and then west into a more rural area of gently rolling countryside. Few houses were visible from the road, and there was little traffic when she turned off at the exit for the prison. A mile later, she drove up to a huge sprawling facility surrounded by high walls with razor wire and guard towers. The mere thought of being confined inside such a bleak place for even one day made Kate's palms sweat and gave her a bad case of claustrophobia.

She parked and approached the main entrance, which appeared to be a tunnel. A uniformed guard with hard eyes and a square jaw stood behind the wire gate.

"I'd like to see one of your inmates," Kate said.

"Visiting days are Saturday, Sunday, and Monday evenings."

"Oh, I didn't know that." Kate chided herself for not checking for the prison's rules on visitors. She glanced around, hoping to find someone to appeal to besides the stoic guard at the gate. "I've come all the way from Copper Mill to see Arthur W. Carew Jr. I believe his ex-wife died recently, and his children—"

"You'll have to come back tomorrow during visiting hours, eight to three fifteen."

She dreaded the thought of driving all the way back home only to return again in the morning. "Surely there's a way I could see Mr. Carew, just for a few moments. It is important. I didn't know there were specific hours."

The guard, his cap squarely on his head, scowled at her. "Look, lady, we got more than twelve hundred prisoners here, and we got rules. You gotta be on the inmate's approved-visitor list and show up during visiting hours."

"Approved list?"

He shoved a form at her through a slot in the fence. "Fill that out. The warden will run a background check and approve you within thirty days."

Thirty days! Good grief! "This really can't wait that long."

"Unless you're a minister or an attorney, those are the rules. You gotta be on the approved-visitor list."

Kate didn't suppose this bored, by-the-book guard would think being a minister's wife qualified her for the exception. But it gave her an idea for a different approach.

She took the form from him. "Thank you. I appreciate that you have a difficult job, and you're only doing what you've been told to do."

His expression softened ever so slightly.

She returned to her car and used her cell phone to place a call to the prison switchboard, asking for a chaplain.

Deacon Moore had a big booming voice capable of reaching the far corners of the biggest church in Nashville without the aid of a microphone.

As succinctly as possible, Kate introduced herself, explained her mission, and why it was urgent she see Wyn Carew.

"That's Wyn Carew, all right. He's one of my boys."

"Thank goodness!" Kate breathed a prayer of thanksgiving.

"He's come a long way since he's been locked up." Deacon Moore's voice held a note of pride. "He doesn't talk about his family much. A lot of the men don't, especially if they don't have contact with them. It's too painful a subject."

"I think his ex-wife cut off all contact between him and the children after the divorce," Kate said.

"I'd say that'd be cruel and unusual punishment for a man like Wyn."

The chaplain grew quiet for a moment. Kate sensed he was thinking how best to approach the situation.

"Tell you what, Mrs. Hanlon. You walk on back to the guard gate. Tell 'em you're here to see me. I'll be there soon as I can locate Wyn and get him on his way to my office. You can meet with him here."

"Thank you, Mr. Moore. I really appreciate your help, and so will the children."

"Call me Deacon, Mrs. Hanlon," he boomed through the phone. "That's what all my flock call me."

Smiling, Kate closed her phone and returned to the guard gate. The guard was none too happy that she'd circumvented the system.

WELL OVER SIX FEET TALL and close to three hundred pounds, Deacon Moore was as big as his voice had implied. He wore his hair cut short, making it look like a fuzzy gray skullcap against his ebony skin. His broad smile revealed one gold tooth, and his dark eyes shone with an inner peace that had to come from deep within his gentle spirit.

He escorted Kate inside the labyrinth of corridors to his office.

"The guard's bringing Wyn in from the fields. He's on the landscaping crew, so it may take him a few minutes to clean up and get here."

"That's fine. I'm just glad that I finally located him." She took a seat at a small conference table at one end of Deacon's office. Except for a wooden cross on one wall, the office was devoid of any decoration.

"Tell me about Wyn," she said.

Deacon sat down at the table opposite her. He didn't appear particularly ministerial in a long-sleeved, maroon turtleneck shirt and dark slacks, but he did have a certain aura of strength that had nothing to do with his muscular physique.

"I'd say he's a model prisoner. Works hard, keeps out of trouble. Attends church services every week. Even got his GED since he's been inside. Lately he's been studying botany and plant propagation."

That sounded ambitious for a man in prison. "What about his drinking? From his conviction, I gather that alcohol was a problem."

"As far as I can tell, he's been clean and sober since he was arrested, and there's more ways to get drugs and alcohol inside a place like this than you'd think. Attends regular AA meetings too. He feels a lot of guilt for what happened."

"Do you think he'd want to have a relationship with his children?"

At the sound of heavy footsteps, Deacon looked past her to the open doorway and stood. "I'll let you ask him yourself."

Kate turned in her chair.

Clean shaven and close to six feet tall, Wyn Carew looked leaner and more fit than he had in the photo Kate had seen. Older too. His tobacco-brown hair had traces of gray, and his face had been etched by the sun and the passage of time.

Dressed in prison stripes, he paused at the doorway, glanced at her, then directed his attention to the chaplain. "You wanted to see me, Deacon?" He spoke in a calm, soft voice that held the same hint of Appalachian roots as Megan's did.

"This is Kate Hanlon from Copper Mill," Deacon explained. "She asked to see you."

He shifted his gaze back to Kate, and his brows drew together in a puzzled frown. "Am I supposed to know you?"

"Not at all. I know your children, though."

Interest sparked in his clear blue eyes, but he seemed to keep his curiosity in check.

"Your children are all fine," she hastened to reassure him. "Until recently, they've been staying with me and my husband. He's the pastor of Faith Briar Church in Copper Mill."

Deacon gestured to the chair at the end of the table. "Have a seat, Wyn."

He eased himself onto the chair. "Where's Glynis? Isn't she with them?"

"She was until a couple months ago. There was an accident, Mr. Carew. I'm sorry to tell you, Glynis Maddock was killed in a car accident." Kate avoided mentioning that the crash was the result of a high-speed police chase. That information could wait.

He stared at her a moment, shock registering in his eyes and an almost imperceptible wince of pain before he scrubbed his hands over his face.

"I haven't talked to Glynis or had any contact since I got the divorce papers from her. I tried writing to her, but after a while, my letters came back as undeliverable." He rested his large hands on the table, studying his short nails and callused palms. "I figured maybe it was better that way. Glynis and the kids could start a new life, find somebody who could do better for them than I could locked up in here."

"I brought a snapshot of the children. I thought you'd like to see how much they've grown." She took the photo from her suit pocket and slid it across the table. "It's not a recent photo. Megan looks more grown up now than in the picture."

With trembling fingers, he pulled the snapshot closer. As though he were afraid to actually touch them, he drew a fingertip across their faces without making contact with the picture. "Becker kind of looks like me, don't you think? Except his hair is a lot lighter than mine ever was. Gwen and Megan both look like their ma."

He looked up at Kate again, tears glistening in his eyes. "What's going to happen to them now?"

"I'm hoping you'll be able to help me with that. Megan didn't know of any relatives who might take them in. I thought perhaps you'd have family who could help out."

Slowly, he shook his head. "I had an aunt and uncle in Kentucky, but they've passed. My folks are long gone too."

Disappointment sucked away Kate's natural optimism.

"It's possible someone in our church might take them in." Offhand, she couldn't think of a family who'd have room for three more youngsters on a permanent basis. The arrangement with Renee certainly wasn't permanent. But somewhere in Copper Mill—

"You've got your first parole hearing next week on Thursday," Deacon said to Wyn.

Wyn glanced toward his pastor, then back to Kate. "Guys don't usually get out on the first try, but Deacon says I might have a shot. Good behavior and all."

"Really? Do you think it's possible?" she asked both men.

Since Wyn was locked in prison, she hadn't really considered that he'd be able to care for his own children. Deacon, as Wyn's pastor, certainly spoke highly of the man. Perhaps . . .

Wyn shrugged, a gesture that mirrored Beck's feigned disinterest when he didn't want to answer a question.

"Parole isn't unheard of under these circumstances," Deacon said. "But in order for the parole board to agree to his release, Wyn would need a sponsor on the outside, a place to live, and a job. I've been working on that, but I admit I haven't made much progress. Even if everything fell into place, it would still take the parole board a month to make a decision after the hearing officer makes his recommendation."

Kate wondered if she and Renee could hold off the social worker from children's services that long.

"I've been trying not to hope too much," Wyn said. "The letdown can get to a man, make him do dumb things that put off his parole that much longer. I don't want to do that. Particularly now when the kids . . ." He looked down at the photo again.

A plan was beginning to take shape in Kate's mind and brought with it a glimmer of hope. "Would you be willing to take care of the children if you were released?"

"Absolutely! They're my kids."

He spoke with such conviction, Kate didn't doubt that he meant what he said. But could Kate trust a man fresh out of prison to be a good parent to three children who didn't even know him?

She decided to let that thought simmer. There were other matters to consider. The diamond thieves were still at large. She didn't want to put the children at greater risk if their father had somehow been involved with the three robbers. "Do you know a Hank Weller?"

He thought for a moment. "Can't say that I do, ma'am."

"What about Perry Weller or Curt Smedley?"

He shook his head. "Why do you ask?"

"Hank Weller was driving the car when your ex-wife died. Turns out he was wanted for armed robbery along with his brother and a third man."

Wyn's hands flexed into fists. "How'd Glynis get messed up with guys like that?"

"That I don't know." She looked to the chaplain. "If I was able to arrange a job for Wyn, a place he could live with the children, and a sponsor, what would the parole board need as proof?"

"Some affidavits signed by a notary public, your sworn testimony, and details of the arrangement. Plus my word that Wyn would do well on the outside, which I'll freely give."

Nodding thoughtfully, she said, "I can't make any promises, but I will do what I can to help you get paroled. But you have to promise me, if I get you out of here, you'll stay sober and take good care of the children."

Wyn sketched an X over his heart. "I swear, ma'am. I've missed my kids so much, but there wasn't much I could do about it. I wouldn't risk losing them again for anything in the world if I somehow get a second chance."

Kate hoped she was being a good judge of his character. The chaplain had given Wyn a good recommendation. She felt she could trust that Deacon had been honest with her.

"Guess you can go on back to work, Wyn," Deacon said. "I'll keep in touch with Mrs. Hanlon."

He stood and looked down at the photo still on the table. "Ma'am, would it be all right if I keep this picture? All these years, I've thought about my kids . . ." His gaze slid away from the snapshot to Kate.

"Of course." Kate quickly pulled one of Paul's business cards from her pocket. "If you'd like to write to the children, you can send it in care of Faith Briar Church. I'll see they get your letter."

The guard who had delivered Wyn to the chaplain's office was waiting for him outside the door.

Kate watched him walk away down the bleak corridor, then turned to thank Deacon for his help. As she left, she knew that if she was going to succeed in getting Wyn released from prison, she had a lot of arrangements to make.

BACK ON THE ROAD HOME, she was about a half hour from Copper Mill when her cell phone chimed. Checking for traffic, she pulled off to the side and answered the call.

"Kate! The children are gone!" Renee's shrill voice announced in a state of panic. "I came to school to pick them up. I've looked everywhere for them. They're not here!"

"Where are you now?"

"I'm still at the school. Kate, I don't know what to do. Umpkins is so worried."

"Call Sheriff Roberts. I'll be there in thirty minutes."

Dear Lord, please let the children be all right.

Chapter Twenty

Breaking every speed law in Tennessee, Kate reached Copper Mill Elementary School in twenty minutes. She pulled up to the curb behind Sheriff Roberts' police cruiser and leaped out of the car.

"Have you found them yet?" she asked as she hurried toward Renee and the sheriff. Skip Spencer was there too, his expression as grim as the others.

"Nobody has seen them," Renee wailed. "I asked everyone. They've vanished. Gone. Oh dear, oh dear, oh dear. Those sweet little children."

"Calm down, Renee," the sheriff ordered. "Hysteria won't get us anywhere."

She sobbed and hiccuped, her eyes frantic.

"Renee, when you brought them to school this morning, were they acting any different than usual?" Kate asked.

"No, no, they were fine. I watched them all the way into the school."

"Skip, go check with the principal," the sheriff said. "Ask her if they made it to all of their classes today. Maybe they ducked out early to go someplace on their own."

As conscientious as Megan was, Kate didn't think the girl would let her siblings ditch school unless there was a compelling reason.

"I'm on it, sir." Skip trotted away.

Sheriff Roberts lifted his hat and resettled it squarely on his head. "The kids have had a pretty upsetting time lately. It's possible they decided to run away."

"They didn't have any money," Kate pointed out.

"Megan wouldn't have left," Renee insisted. "She was so excited about selling her cornhusk dolls at the Old Timer's Day event. She spent all afternoon yesterday working on the cutest little doll. She even made the doll a fancy hat and a sparkly necklace. Said it reminded her of me. Wasn't that sweet?" Renee lost it again and started sobbing even more loudly than before. She was so distraught, she'd left Kisses in his tote in her car. The poor little thing yipped, trying to get his mistress' attention.

"Sheriff, I really don't think Megan would run away with her brother and sister. She tried to support them before and found out how difficult it is to earn enough money to keep them fed." Worry and fear burned in Kate's stomach. "I'm far more concerned that the diamond thieves kidnapped them."

The sheriff shook his head. "I know you're worried about those crooks, but let's not jump to conclusions too fast."

"The thieves want those diamonds," Kate insisted. "They think, wrongly, that the children know where they are."

Skip came trotting back. "Mrs. Walner said school let out early for a teacher's-training thing. All the kids went home at two o'clock."

Renee's eyes widened. "I didn't know that. No one told me to pick them up early."

"Maybe the kids decided to walk home," the sheriff suggested. "Or go to Emma's for an ice cream. They'll probably turn up."

Kate wasn't so sure. "It's only a few blocks to Renee's house. Try calling your mother, Renee. See if they've shown up at your house."

Renee's hand was shaking so badly, she had to punch in her home number twice. Her mother reported that she hadn't seen the children.

"Your house is closer, Miz Hanlon. Maybe they walked there," Skip suggested.

Digging her phone out of her handbag, Kate called Paul. He was at the church and promised to run over to the house to check for the children. He'd let her know if he found them.

"Tell you what, Kate." The sheriff rubbed at his cheek. "Skip and I will check here in town, including Emma's Ice Cream."

"Steve's gift shop too," Kate added. "Megan might have wanted to talk to him about Old Timer's Day."

"Good idea," he agreed. "And I'll check their old place in Smoky Mountain Hollow. They might have decided to go back to their old trailer for some reason. You and Renee can go on home. We'll let you know just as soon as we find them."

Kate wasn't happy with that decision. She planned to look for the kids everywhere she could think of in town. Still, her instinct told her that they'd been kidnapped by Perry Weller and Curt Smedley. She sincerely hoped she was wrong.

Driving slowly, she wove her way up one street and down another through town, hoping to catch a glimpse of the kids. On a hunch, she stopped at the library.

Livvy was at her desk poring over what appeared to be a computer printout.

Kate rapped on her open office door. "Livvy, have you seen Megan Maddock this afternoon? The girl I was in here with last week?"

The librarian looked at Kate over the top of her reading glasses. "I haven't noticed her. You might ask the boys in the back. They've been eyeballing every girl that's come in today. Is something wrong?"

"I'll tell you later." Kate quickly walked to the back of the library, where three young adolescent boys were pretending to study, one of them the young man who'd done a double take of Megan after her beauty-shop makeover.

"Have you fellows seen Megan Maddock this afternoon?" Kate asked.

Two boys shook their heads, but the third spoke up. "I saw her out front of school after we got out."

"Yeah, Boyd's got a crush on Megan," one of the other boys teased, wiggling his eyebrows.

"This is important, please. Boyd, when you saw Megan, was she with anyone?"

Boyd shrugged and tried to look like he didn't care. "Her little sister and brother, like always."

"Was there anyone else with them? Someone in a car or a van she could've gotten into?"

He slanted a glance toward his buddies. "Maybe there was a van. One of the moms picking up their kid, probably."

Kate's chest tightened. "What color was the van you saw?"

"I dunno."

One of his buddies gave Boyd an elbow jab. "Boydie-boy only has eyes for Megan," he sing-songed.

Boyd jabbed his friend back. "Light colored. Maybe like a really light brown or something. I dunno."

Her heart sinking, Kate asked, "Did you see her get into the van? Or who was driving it?"

"Naw. Me and my friends were coming over here to the library. We've gotta wait here till our moms get home from work. I wasn't paying that much attention, you know?"

His buddy snorted at that and smirked.

"It's all right, Boyd. Thank you for your help."

Kate hurried back outside. While standing on the sidewalk, she used her cell phone to call the sheriff. The operator agreed to put her through to Sheriff Roberts' cell phone.

While she waited for him to answer, Kate looked up and down the street in the futile hope that she'd spot Megan strolling along, oblivious that everyone was looking for her.

The sheriff answered. "Kate, did you locate the kids?"

"No." She told him about the van that Boyd had seen.

"I've already got an APB out on that van. I'll get some of my men from the other district offices searching this part of the county."

"They have a two-hour head start on us." Kate's voice shook with anxiety. "They could be all the way to Knoxville by now. Or Chattanooga. There are a million places they could hide out where we'd never find them."

"If it's Weller and his buddy, they want something. They'll get in touch. You can count on it."

That thought did little to reassure Kate.

As she scoured the streets of Copper Mill in her car, she prayed that she was wrong about the kidnapping. Even responsible kids could do crazy things, like go home with a friend and forget to tell anyone, or decide to play at the park and let the time slip by.

As much as she prayed for the best, she kept her eye out for a light-colored van.

With each passing minute, she grew more and more anxious, as though the heavy beat of an anvil were marking time. Having a child kidnapped was a parent's worst nightmare, and it was no less frightening for Kate even though she hadn't given birth to Megan, Gwen, and Beck.

To the West, the setting sun speared the sky with streaks of red and orange like fiery daggers. In mere moments, it would be dark. Thoughts of them, frightened and hungry, pummeled Kate, but she sought solace in the knowledge that the Lord would look after them.

With little awareness of where she was, she pulled into the Faith Briar Church parking lot and got out of the car. A pair of bats darted through the twilight sky, and a bird sang his evening song.

Inside, the church was dark. Kate didn't bother to turn on the lights. Instead, she slipped into a pew in the back. Tears of fear and fatigue slid down her cheeks. "Our Father, which art in—"

Her phone chimed.

Frantically, she dug her phone out of her handbag and

flipped it open. The screen glowed brightly in the darkness but gave no clue as to the caller.

"Hello?"

"Miz Hanlon. It's me. Megan."

Thank you, Lord! "Where are you, Megan? Are you all right?"

Megan screamed.

"Megan? What's happening?"

"She's fine." A deep male voice cut in. "Her kid sister and brother are too. But they won't be for long if you don't do exactly as I tell you."

Kate forced herself to remain calm. "What is it you want?"

"Only what's ours." The caller's voice seemed to sneer at her through the satellite connection. "We want our diamonds."

"I have no idea where—"

"Find 'em, or these kids will end up at the bottom of the lake with a rock tied to their ankles. You got that?"

Kate swallowed hard. How could this be happening on the very day she had located the children's father? "I understand."

"Good. Now listen carefully. Tomorrow at noon, I want you to deliver the diamonds to the public park in McGhee. You know where that is?"

"I know where McGhee is." Her voice shook. "Halfway to Knoxville. But I don't know where the park is."

"You'll find it. There's a trash can outside the restroom. Drop the bag of diamonds in there, then get back in your car and drive away."

"But I'm telling you, I don't have any idea where the diamonds are," she protested. "And I'm not going to deliver anything to you unless—"

"If you want the kids back safe, you'd better find the diamonds, lady. If you don't deliver the goods by noon, my partner will drop the first kid into the lake."

"Please. The children are innocent."

"Noon tomorrow. Come alone, and no cops. I'll be watching, and if I see anything that looks like a cop, these three brats are goners. Got that?"

"I understand, but please—"

He broke the connection.

Kate stared at the glowing screen, trying to figure out what to do. She couldn't give the robbers diamonds she didn't have and didn't know how to find. She and Sheriff Roberts had searched the same trailer the thieves had. And if the children knew where the diamonds were, surely they would have told Weller and his partner in order to save themselves.

Snapping the phone closed, she stood on legs as wobbly as those of a newborn filly.

Kate drove her car the short distance home and parked in the garage. Paul met her at the door into the house.

"Have the kids turned up yet?" he asked.

She walked past him into the living room.

He followed her. "Kate, what's wrong? You're as pale as a ghost, honey."

Unsure what to do, she simply came to a stop in the middle of the huge room. "They've been kidnapped."

"What?"

He took her into his arms and held her close until she was able to stop weeping and tell him about the phone call.

"You have to call the sheriff," Paul said when she finished.

She looked up into his clear blue eyes and saw her own fear mirrored there. "They said no cops."

"Since we don't know where the diamonds are, they may hurt the children anyway. Sheriff Roberts will know what to do."

She glanced at her watch. Almost eight o'clock. In only sixteen hours, Weller and Smedley would start drowning the children she loved, and there was nothing she could do to stop them.

She'd have to call the sheriff. But just as important, she *had* to find the diamonds.

Chapter Twenty-One

K ate barely closed her eyes all night. Though she tried not to disturb Paul's sleep, she knew he was restless too.

She relived her conversation with the kidnappers and mentally repeated every word Renee and the sheriff had said when they'd discovered the children were missing. Something Renee had said niggled at the back of her mind, but she was so distracted by the need to rescue the children that she wasn't able to recall it.

As slanting rays of sun crept into the bedroom, she remembered yet again how the kidnapper had threatened to throw the children in a lake if she didn't comply and bring him the diamonds. But which lake? Tennessee had hundreds of lakes.

Vaguely she recalled the snapshot of Glynis and her boyfriend standing in front of a log cabin. Where had Megan said that picture was taken?

"Tellico Lake!" she said out loud.

Paul mumbled, "What about Tellico?"

"That's got to be where the children are. I need to go to Renee's house and look at the snapshots she gave to Megan to put together in a scrapbook." She rolled out of bed and started to get dressed. Megan might not have put the photo of her mother and Hank in the scrapbook itself, but she wouldn't have thrown it away.

Paul sat up. "You're going now? Renee won't be up at this hour."

"She will be when I get there." Pulling on jeans and a sweatshirt, Kate found her sneakers and slipped her feet into them. "I'll call you if I find out anything."

She dashed out to the Honda and drove through the empty streets of Copper Mill, coming to a halt in front of Renee's house.

At the front door, she had to ring the doorbell twice before she heard Renee moving around inside.

Renee looked through the peephole, then threw the door open. "Have you found the children? I haven't slept a wink all night. Not a wink."

"No, we haven't found the children, and I'm sorry to bother you so early, Renee. But it's important."

"Of course. If it will help get those babies back safely."

Kate slipped past Renee. "I think I know where Megan and the other children are being held. I need to take a look at Megan's scrapbook. Do you know where she keeps it?"

"I suppose it's in the guest room where she and Gwen are staying." She pointed toward the back of the house. "She's a real neat and tidy girl. Gwen too. They're so sweet—" A sob cut off Renee's voice.

Not waiting for Renee to show her the way, Kate hurried down the hallway.

The guest room was beautifully made up, with an antique double bed covered in a handmade quilt with a traditional diamond design in shades of aqua and pink. Curtains picked up the colors in a floral pattern, and both the quilt and curtains were striking in contrast to the white walls.

Kate halted in the doorway. "Do you have any idea where the girls are keeping their things?" She didn't want to go plowing through Renee's possessions.

"I made room in the closet for their hanging things. They're using the right-hand drawers of the dresser too. I have to say, for two little girls, they don't own much of a wardrobe."

The distressed walnut dresser—with a fancy cornhusk doll propped in front of the mirror—was a lovely piece of furniture Kate normally would have taken time to admire. But she didn't have time now to consider anything except finding the children.

She started by opening each drawer and feeling around inside. Brushes and combs. Hair bows. Underwear. Socks. T-shirts. No scrapbook.

Where did you put the scrapbook, Megan?

Kate tried the closet next. There were scuffed tennis shoes on the floor, plus the two suitcases Kate had loaned the children. The box of cornhusks made the closet smell a bit musty.

Please, Lord, help me out here.

Then Kate spotted the scrapbook on the top shelf. She pulled it down and sat on the edge of the bed to look through the pages. She was pretty sure Megan wouldn't include the photo of Hank Weller on the pages that contained better memories, but when she turned to the back of the book, she found what she was looking for: Hank and Glynis standing in front of a log cabin.

"Is that what you were after?" Renee asked.

"Yes." Kate held up the snapshot for Renee to see. "This was taken at Tellico Lake. Now all I have to do is find this particular cabin, and I'll be able to bring the children home safe and sound."

"Tellico's a fair-sized lake."

"Which means there are many miles of shoreline." Leaving Kate looking for the proverbial needle in a haystack. "I think the cabin must be near McGhee."

"That's not much to go on." Renee sat down next to Kate on the bed to get a better look at the picture.

"Would you say this snapshot was taken morning or afternoon?" Kate eyed the shadows cast by the cabin and the trees behind it.

"No way to tell, is there?"

"I'm thinking the cabin faces the lake. The sky is clear. Most of the time, clouds build up around here during the afternoon. These shadows are pretty long, so it's got to be early morning."

"You could be right, I suppose. But I don't know how that helps you find the youngsters."

Holding on to the snapshot, Kate set the scrapbook aside. "It tells me the cabin is on the west side of the lake, and it's somewhere near McGhee."

"You still don't know exactly where."

"When I get to McGhee, I'll find someone who recognizes the cabin. Then we'll know exactly where they are." She counted the remaining hours until the time she was supposed to deliver the diamonds. "I hope." *And pray the Lord will lead me.*

"I'll go with you," Renee announced. "It'll just take me a minute to—"

"No, Renee. It might be dangerous. Besides, I may be way off track. You should stay here where the children can find you if they get free of their kidnappers."

Renee objected, but Kate didn't have time to argue.

Back in the car, Kate placed a call to Sheriff Roberts and told him what she was doing.

"These characters could be dangerous, Kate."

"I'll be careful," she replied.

"We've got a female FBI agent in McGhee. She's going to impersonate you and drop a bag of fake diamonds in the park's trash can. We'll tail whoever picks up the phony diamonds, and he'll lead us to the children."

"What if Weller realizes the diamonds are fake or spots your people following him?" she asked. "The children would be at even greater risk."

"It's a good plan, Kate. The FBI agents know what they're doing."

As Kate headed north on the highway, she hoped Sheriff Roberts was right. But if she was able to locate where the kidnappers were holding the children, the FBI could step in to rescue them that much sooner.

She glanced at her watch. Less than three hours until the diamond drop was scheduled to take place.

Her mouth was dry, her palms sweaty. As she peered through the windshield at the passing scenery, her pulse accelerated. Nerves had her stomach tied in a knot.

Please, Lord . . .

The wildflowers growing alongside the road were buffeted by the wakes of passing cars, delicate yellow and blue blossoms whipping back and forth, yet they withstood the onslaught. The Maddock children had remained steady despite circumstances that might have broken other youngsters.

A sign appeared for the town of McGhee, and she turned off the highway onto a narrow blacktop road. The intersection boasted a service station, a small diner, and a convenience store that offered fresh bait along with milk and eggs. She decided to make her first stop at the convenience store.

A heavyset woman somewhere between the age of fifty and seventy sat on a stool behind the counter. A small black-and-white TV nearby was tuned to a sports highlights show. A half-eaten candy bar rested on the counter.

"Excuse me," Kate said. "I wonder if you can help me."

The woman's gaze slid from the TV to Kate. "Sure. What kin I do for you?"

"I'm coming to visit a friend at her cabin somewhere near here, but I'm afraid I didn't get very good directions." Kate held up the snapshot. "I'm hoping you'll recognize the place and can tell me how to get there."

Squinting at the photo, the woman shook her head. "Don't look familiar to me, but I live over in Sweetwater. Don't spend much time at the lake. Got work 'n got grandkids to fuss over."

"I see. Well . . . is there a road that goes along the shoreline?"

"Sure. You jes' keep headin' down this road a piece." She

thumbed toward the lake. "Go through town, and you'll end up at the boat ramp. Turn jes' before you get there. That's Lake Front Road, and it'll take you along this side of the lake."

Kate thanked the woman for her time and returned to her car. Even though the clerk hadn't been able to reduce the size of the haystack Kate was searching, Kate knew she was getting close when she drove by a small park in the middle of town. Some kids were playing on the swings, and a pickup softball game was in progress in a grassy area of the park.

She wondered if one or more of the players were undercover FBI agents or sheriff's deputies. There was no sign of a white or beige van.

She turned right just before the boat ramp and public parking area. Houses were set back from the street on both sides of the road, some of them hidden by thickets of wild blackberry bushes; the most prominent sign of residents, the mailboxes with rural-route numbers, marked each driveway.

Driving slowly, she checked the driveways for a light-colored van. In her head, the minutes were ticking down one by one, fraying her already strained nerves.

Spotting a mail truck making deliveries, she caught up and parked in front of the truck, leaving the motor running. She hopped out of the car and hurried back to speak to the mail carrier.

"I wonder if you can help me." She held out the snapshot to the man, who looked to be in his thirties. His short-sleeved uniform shirt was open at the collar, revealing a sparkling white T-shirt. "I'm looking for this particular house. Do you recognize it? I think it's somewhere nearby."

He studied the photo. "I'm not sure, ma'am. Some of the houses on the lakeside you can't even see from the road. Those that are summer places like this one don't get much mail."

"Please, it's important. Does the cabin look at all familiar?"

He scratched his jaw and handed the picture back to Kate. "I can't be sure, ma'am, but it looks like a place about a mile up the road. 'Course, that picture was taken on the back side of the house, the lakeside. I've only seen the front of the place, but it's got logs like that."

Kate felt a surge of hope. "Do you remember the number of the house?"

"Oh, gosh, ma'am . . ." He looked off into the distance. "Could be around 2211 or 2215. I can't be sure."

Kate thanked the young man and dashed back to her car. She shifted into gear and sped up the road, catching quick glimpses of the numbers on the mailboxes. As the numbers got closer to what she was looking for, she slowed, peering down each driveway in search of the telltale van.

When she looked back to the road, she saw two children running toward her waving their hands over their heads, trying to attract attention.

Her heart skipped a beat. *Gwen and Beck!*

Chapter Twenty-Two

K ate slammed on the brakes, jammed the gearshift into Park, and leaped out of the car. She ran toward the children.

"Gwen! Beck! Are you all right? Where's Megan? I've been frantic with worry." The two youngsters flew into her arms, and she hugged them.

"Miz Hanlon! Miz Hanlon!"

"Two bad men took us. I didn't wanna go," Beck said.

"Megan helped us climb out a window." Trembling, Gwen pressed her face against Kate's shoulder.

"I wasn't scared. Megan said it'd be all right." Beck's chin quivered as he put up a brave front.

Relief and gratitude poured through Kate as she soothed her hand over the child's blond hair and caught a whiff of little-boy sweat. "I'm sure you were a very brave boy. Where's Megan now?"

"I think the man caught her before she got out. She told us to run like the wind when we got outside, so we did."

"Megan boosted us up to a high window in the bedroom."
Visibly frightened, Gwen looked back the way they had come.
"We couldn't reach it on our own. She was 'posed to come
right after us."

"I hurt my knee when I fell."

A quick glance told Kate that he'd ripped his jeans as well
as scraping his knee.

"We'll get you fixed up when we get home, Beck. Let's
all get into my car now. I need to tell the sheriff you're all
right."

"Shouldn't we wait for Megan?" Gwen asked.

"How far down the road is the cabin where those men
took you?"

Looking anxious, the child hesitated. "Right up there where
that big hangy-down tree is." Clearly the weeping willow drap-
ing over the roadway was too close for Gwen's comfort.

For Kate's too.

Urging the children toward the car, Kate said, "We'll keep
an eye out for Megan while we wait for the police to come
help us."

"Can't we go get her?" Gwen pleaded.

"Not right now. She'll be all right." *Kate hoped*.

The two youngsters climbed into the backseat of the car
and held each other. The sight of the two frightened children
trying to comfort one another nearly broke Kate's heart.

She plucked the cell phone from her handbag and called
Sheriff Roberts.

"I'm in McGhee," Kate announced. "Beck and Gwen managed to get away from the kidnappers, and I have them in the

car with me," Kate told him. "The kidnappers still have Megan, though."

"Okay, hang on. I'll try to patch you through to the FBI on the scene in McGhee."

The phone went silent for a few achingly long moments, then she heard a male voice.

"Mrs. Hanlon? This is Agent Turner."

"Yes, sir."

"I understand you have the two younger children with you."

"Yes, sir. We're in my car."

"Exactly what is your current location?"

"I'm on Lake Front Road a few miles north of McGhee." She gave him the number on the nearest mailbox. "I'm only a few houses from where the kidnappers are still holding Megan, the oldest girl. It's just up the road, but I can't see the cabin from where I'm parked."

"All right. I want you to stay out of sight. It's almost time for the ransom drop at the park. We'll close in on whoever shows up and then get some men to that location."

"But with two of the children escaping, they may forget about the diamonds and make a run for it," Kate protested. "They could hold Megan hostage."

"I'll send a car as soon as I can." With that, Agent Turner disconnected.

"Can we go get Megan now?" Beck asked.

"The FBI wants us to wait for them to get here." Kate eyed the driveway just past the weeping willow. "When you got away from the cabin, were there one or two men inside?"

"Just the ugly one," Beck answered.

"The other man went away and said he'd be back soon."

"Did he leave in a car?" Kate asked.

"Yeah, a big black car," Gwen said.

"An old one that rattled," Beck added.

Still watching the driveway, Kate called Sheriff Roberts again and told him about the car. He said he'd pass the word on to the FBI so they could be on the lookout for the vehicle sent to pick up the diamonds at the park.

When Kate snapped her phone closed, she felt a surge of impatience. She was afraid that with the younger children escaping, the remaining thief would make a break for it before the FBI could get there. He could easily take Megan with him as a shield.

She opened the car door. "I want to see what's going on at the cabin. You two stay in the car, ducked down and out of sight. And no matter what, keep the doors locked. Do you understand?"

Gwen nodded. "Be careful, Miz Hanlon."

Kate glanced down the road back toward town. No sign of the police or the FBI yet.

Turning toward the cabin, she stayed near the edge of the road where she couldn't be seen. The neighborhood of scattered houses and cabins seemed eerily quiet for a spring day. No children played in the sheltered yards. No bikes had been left abandoned in view of the street. Either these were summer homes not yet open for the season or the occupants were all enjoying their view of the lakefront.

When she reached the driveway, she checked again for oncoming cars, hoping to see flashing red lights. Lake Front Road was as empty as the nearby yards.

She peered down the driveway. A tan van was parked close to the house.

As she stood spying on the cabin, a man shoved Megan out the front door and down the steps to the van. Kate recognized Perry Weller from his booking photo.

"You're comin' with me, missy," he ordered. "Don't even try to get away, or I'll knock you senseless."

Kate's breath lodged in her lungs. She had to think fast. She couldn't let Perry drive away with Megan. No telling what he would do to her, or if the FBI would ever be able to find her.

Kate stepped into full view. "Yoo-hoo! Hello there. I wonder if you can help me." She walked down the middle of the driveway.

Weller's head snapped around. "We don't want anything."

Recognition sparked in Megan's eyes. She started to say something, then thought better of it and closed her mouth.

Kate kept walking. "I'm looking for Mary Jane Bulenski's cabin. She invited me to visit for the weekend."

"She ain't here." Perry gave Megan a shove into the van.

"Do you know which cabin is hers?" Kate persisted, praying the FBI would show up soon.

"I don't know nothin' about a Bulenski. Now get out of my way, or I'll run over you."

Kate held her ground and kept talking. "Could you give me a ride into town? My car broke down a ways back. I'm going to need a tow."

Ignoring her, Perry climbed into the van. At the same time,

the door on the opposite side of the vehicle opened. Megan jumped out and started running.

"Hey, you little—" Perry swung out of the van, shaking his fist at Megan. "Come back here!"

"Run, Megan!" Kate yelled.

She caught up with Megan and grabbed her hand as they both ran for the road. Behind her, Kate heard the van's engine start. The wheels crunched on the gravel driveway, coming fast. They'd never be able to outrun the van.

"Into the bushes," Kate ordered.

They moved into the undergrowth. Their feet sank into the soft ground. Whiplike branches flayed at their faces as they ran parallel to the road, angling toward the spot where Kate had parked her car. They ducked under pine trees. Drooping branches without needles seemed to reach out to snare them like witches' fingers.

"Did you find Gwen and Beck?" Megan asked as they ran.

"They're in my car. Hurry."

Kate ventured a look behind her. Perry wasn't following them on foot. *Thank goodness!*

Then she heard the van again. On the road. Perry was watching for them to pop out of the woods. He intended to capture Megan again. And Kate.

Worse, Kate was leading Perry directly to Gwen and Beck hiding in her car.

"Stop. Wait." Kate was breathing heavily. Her lungs burned. She didn't know which way to turn. *Please, Lord . . .*

Then through the trees, she saw the flash of red lights and heard the sudden wail of a siren. A black-and-white police cruiser appeared on the road right in front of the van. Moments later, a second police car arrived from the opposite direction, trapping Perry Weller between them.

Kate sank to her knees on the damp ground in gratitude and thanksgiving.

SEVERAL HOURS LATER, after giving the police their statements, Kate and the three children were at Renee's house being thoroughly pampered with ice cream and cake served on elegant china at the dining-room table.

Kate chose a nice soothing tea over the soft drinks the youngsters preferred.

"I simply can't get over how brave you all were," Renee said.

Caroline, Renee's mother, firmly tapped her cane on the floor to draw everyone's attention. "I say Mayor Briddle should give Kate an award for rescuing our dear children."

Kate sipped a bit of her tea. "I suspect Agent Turner would disagree. He made it clear he thought I was more foolish than brave."

"Pshaw!" Caroline discounted the FBI agent with a wave of her hand. "Men always want to take the credit when it's we women who do all the heavy lifting."

"Well," Kate said, "I for one was more than grateful when his men showed up to bail us out of a tight spot."

"You were great, Miz Hanlon." Scooping the last of her ice cream out of the bowl, Megan grinned across the table at Kate. "I thought I'd bust something when I saw you walkin' down that driveway like you were just passing by."

Looking up from his cake and ice cream, his mouth

smeared with chocolate, Beck said, "I think Megan ought to get a medal too."

"I think we'd all agree with that, Beck." Looping her arm around his narrow shoulders, Kate gave him a hug. "In fact, I think you all deserve a reward for helping to catch those thieves."

Megan brightened. "Is there really a reward?"

"Oh, I don't know, honey. No one has said anything about that."

"Which reminds me," Renee said. "Megan, why don't you show Kate your pretty cornhusk doll? It's so precious, I may have to buy it myself."

Kate recalled the doll she'd seen on the dresser in Megan's room and smiled to herself. She had the feeling the missing diamonds were very close at hand.

Leisurely, Megan got up from the table and went down the hallway to the bedroom. A few moments later, she returned with her doll and placed it in front of Kate.

"Megan, this is beautifully made."

Megan had fashioned a bonnet out of blue fabric and made a matching dress, accessorizing the outfit with a neck-lace made of what appeared to be tiny bits of clear glass glued onto a narrow strip of ribbon.

Intrigued, Kate leaned closer. The bits of glass reflected the light from the overhead chandelier, the facets sparkling with color and brightness, just as she had expected.

"Megan, honey, where did you get these little bits?" Kate asked.

"I didn't take any of your stained glass," she responded

quickly. "They're just some old glass pieces I found in Beck's marble bag at the bottom of my cornhusk box. I didn't think—"

"You found my marbles?" Beck asked. "I've been lookin' everywhere for those."

"Your marbles weren't in the bag, squirt. Just the glass pieces. You probably lost your marbles to some kid at school."

"Didn't." Beck stuck his chin out at a stubborn angle. "If you got my marbles, I want 'em back!"

"Hold on." Kate raised her hand to stop the bickering. "Megan, why don't you bring the bag in here, and we'll all take a look at what you've found."

"They're not worth anything," Megan protested. "Beck's just being—"

She looked at Kate, and Kate saw realization spark in the girl's eyes.

"What is it?" Renee asked. "Do you two know something I don't?"

Grinning, Kate said, "I think Megan has made a grand discovery."

Whirling away from the table, Megan raced back to the bedroom. She returned with a blue denim bag tied around the top with an old, frayed rope.

"That's mine!" Beck reached across the table.

"Let's see what we've got here." Taking the bag from Megan, Kate opened it and slid the contents on a forest green linen napkin she'd spread out on the table.

Dozens of sparkling diamonds spilled out, sized from tiny baguettes to multicarat stones, each worth a small fortune.

Beck frowned and looked disappointed. "Those aren't my marbles."

Stunned, Megan sat down heavily in her chair. "They're diamonds, aren't they?"

"Yes, I believe they are, honey."

"Oh dear, oh dear." Renee fluttered her fingers in the air. "You're going to have to charge more than sixty dollars for your doll, dear. Much more."

Kate laughed. "Megan may want to switch the diamonds for some of my stained glass. She'll still be able to ask quite a bit for the doll."

Continuing to stare at the diamonds, Megan said, "How did those get in with my cornhusks?"

"And in my marble bag?" Beck added.

Kate thought she knew the answer. "After the car crash, the police searched the car. The only unusual thing they found was a bag of marbles."

"Mine?"

"Probably," Kate said. "I'm guessing your mother knew the diamonds were stolen. Hank wanted to take them with him to Nashville, possibly to fence them to a dealer. Maybe he'd hidden them in the bottom of your cornhusk box all along. But your mother knew that Hank's brother was after him to get the diamonds. She switched the diamonds for the marbles and went off with Hank, hoping that you three children would be safe and that Hank's brother would chase after them to Nashville and not bother you."

"But her plan went wrong when the police tried to stop Hank for speeding, and he crashed the car," Renee concluded.

Tears filmed Gwen's eyes. "Ma tried to save us, didn't she?"

Sympathy filled Kate's heart. "Yes, I think she did. She obviously loved you very much."

"Could the mayor give Ma an award for being brave too?" Gwen asked.

Barely able to speak, Kate said, "I think your mother's biggest reward, the only one she really wanted, was to know that her children were safe."

Chapter Twenty-Three

By Monday morning, everyone had heard about Kate's adventures with the diamond thieves. Based on several congratulatory phone calls she'd received, the story had reached epic proportions, the details exaggerated until Kate had single-handedly captured a ring of international diamond thieves that even Interpol had failed to track down.

She simply wanted her life to get back to normal as quickly as possible. Although she had to admit, her "normal" life in Copper Mill always seemed to involve mysteries she felt compelled to solve.

After Paul left for his morning run, Kate dressed in a pair of slacks and a blouse, then drove to Jenkins Nursery. She intended to convince Floyd Jenkins to hire Wyn when he was released from prison.

A young woman in her twenties was working the cash register, assisting a woman whose shopping cart was loaded with bedding plants. The Help Wanted sign still hung on the wall behind the register.

Kate wandered past the display of indoor plants and then went outside in search of Floyd. She found him moving newly arrived pots of azaleas and colorful buddleia butterfly from a cart to a display bench. In his fifties, Floyd wore Bermuda-length khaki shorts and a forest green shirt with the nursery logo on the pocket. His legs were deeply tanned, as was his face.

"Good morning, Mrs. Hanlon. Can I help you find something today?" His pleasant smile emphasized permanent squint lines radiating from the corners of his brown eyes.

"Actually, I'm hoping you're still looking to hire more workers for the nursery." At his stunned expression, she hastened to add, "I have a friend who would be interested."

Embarrassed, he grinned. "I thought for a minute you were applying for the job. Though I'd be happy to hire you, nursery work means a lot of heavy lifting."

"Thanks anyway. I think I'll stick with being a minister's wife. My friend, however, is more than strong enough for the job and experienced in landscaping."

"Oh?" Floyd removed his heavy work gloves and set them on the cart. "Well, send him around. I'll talk to him."

"That's a bit of a problem. He's currently in prison and has his first parole hearing this Thursday. In order to be released, he needs to have a job lined up as well as a place to live."

Concern furrowed Floyd's forehead. "I don't know, Mrs. Hanlon. A couple of times I've taken a chance on an ex-con, and it hasn't worked out real well. They're not happy with the money I pay them, which is the going wage around here, and they stop showing up."

"Wyn Carew is highly motivated. He has three children

whom he's never really had a chance to get to know. They just lost their mother in a car accident." Kate didn't feel it necessary to go into the details of the police chase or the diamond theft. None of that was Wyn's fault or the children's. "If he doesn't get parole, the children will probably be put into foster care and will very likely be separated. They're wonderful kids. I don't want to see that happen to them."

"A man who's been in prison a long time may not be an ideal parent for young children."

"It's a legitimate concern. But the prison chaplain vouches for Wyn. I've met and talked with him. I think he's worth taking a chance on. I know the children are."

Floyd sat down on the edge of his cart and scratched his head. "You say he has landscaping experience?"

Kate knew she had him now. All she'd have to do was get a notarized statement from Floyd that a job would be waiting for Wyn when he was released from prison. She'd even checked to find the closest notary in Pine Ridge.

By LUNCHTIME, she had a letter on Jenkins Nursery letterhead, confirming that Floyd would hire Wyn Carew at a suitable hourly rate of pay. She'd then cajoled the notary to come to the nursery to witness Floyd's signature, since Floyd couldn't leave his place of business until after closing that evening.

With one hurdle met and overcome, she made a quick stop to see Sheriff Roberts. He agreed to talk to the county probation department about Wyn and the plan Kate was putting together for his release from prison. After that, she headed back to Copper Mill.

Although Wyn and the children could possibly move into the old trailer, the thieves had thoroughly trashed it. She wanted the family to be able to start fresh.

She'd have to ask the sheriff to notify the owner of the trailer that it was now vacant. She had other plans for the Maddock family.

THE PLATE-GLASS WINDOW of Cumberland Realty featured flyers for a dozen current listings, with photos of the properties and brief descriptions. Gail Carson was the primary listing agent for almost all of the properties.

The bell over the office door tinkled as Kate stepped inside.

Tracy, a young receptionist with bleached-blonde hair, greeted Kate from behind a desk piled high with file folders and photos of houses.

"Good morning, Mrs. Hanlon. I hear you rounded up an international diamond smuggling ring from South Africa!"

Kate winced. "Not quite. The two thieves who were arrested were very much homegrown and completely ordinary crooks."

The young woman's eager expression collapsed into disappointment.

"I'd like to see Gail for a few minutes, if she's free," Kate said.

She glanced toward the plate-glass wall that separated Gail Carson's office from the reception area. The plucked and polished Realtor was on the phone, her mouth moving, but no sound escaped through the heavy plate glass.

Tracy checked the phone on her desk, where a red light

indicated that someone was on the line. "Mrs. Carson will be right out."

When she got off the phone, Gail immediately stepped out of her office. The picture of professionalism in her pastel blue suit and perfectly coifed hair, Gail extended her hand. She had a grip that communicated she was in charge.

Kate explained what she had in mind. Within moments, Gail had described a cabin that was available for a modest rental. Kate eagerly agreed to take a look at the property.

Gail's shiny black Lexus was parked behind Cumberland Realty. The interior was warm, the leather seats hot from the car sitting in the sun.

Gail turned off the main road, taking a route that wound up the hillside. At a break in the trees, she turned right and pulled up in front of a log cabin that looked as though it had come right out of the Daniel Boone era. Matching windows framed the doorway, and a chimney made of river rock rose above the sloped roof. Off to the side, a rope swing with a tire hung from a high branch of an oak tree.

"There's running water and electricity," Gail announced. "Only one bath, though. The owners added that about ten years ago. Used to be just an outhouse."

Just as the Realtor unlocked the cabin door, her cell phone chimed. She took the call while standing outside, which gave Kate a chance to wander through the cabin on her own.

The great room was sparsely furnished, but a dramatic rock fireplace made up for other amenities that were lacking. The bedrooms were small, closet space minimal. But what

Kate saw in the kitchen gave her hope that Wyn and his children could build their new lives in the cabin. Hanging above the stove was a framed cross-stitched scene of Jesus surrounded by children. As basic as the cabin was, the small piece of art told Kate that the building could become a home.

Gail strolled into the living room, making little effort to hide her dismay. "Not exactly five stars, I'm afraid."

"With a few personal touches and lots of love, I think this will be a perfect home for Mr. Carew and his children."

By Tuesday, on behalf of Wyn Carew, Kate had a signed and notarized rental agreement with the special notation that the contract would be confirmed by Wyn at the time of his release from prison. Some of the church ladies had volunteered to spruce up the cabin with fresh linens and new curtains. Faith Freezer would stock the pantry with enough food to get the family started.

Kate had also arranged with Bernie at the local body shop to let Wyn borrow an old car until he could buy one of his own.

Now, if only the hearing officer and the parole board would cooperate when they heard Wyn's case on Thursday.

She returned home from her errands at about four o'clock to find Paul supervising the kids' kite-building project. He had arranged for Renee to drop them off at the Hanlons', and he promised to bring them home when they'd completed their kites.

Megan, Gwen, and Beck were seated around the dining table putting the finishing touches on kites they'd decorated with crayons or acrylic paints.

"Hey, Miz Hanlon." Interrupting her effort to fasten the kite spine and spar together at right angles, Megan looked up and smiled. She'd drawn a bright yellow stylized sun in the center of her kite. "We're gonna try out the kites when they're finished."

"Bet mine goes the highest." Beck had a forest scene on his kite, all browns and shades of green, with a touch of blue for the sky.

Paul tousled the boy's hair, then turned to Kate. "You got a letter at the church today," he said. "I put it on the dresser in our bedroom."

"Oh?" It was unusual for her to get mail in care of Faith Briar Church. Usually letters addressed to her arrived at the house.

"I thought you might want to open it privately. The return address is Turney Center Industrial Prison."

"Oh!" Understanding dawned, and she glanced at the children. The letter was from either their father or the prison chaplain. "I'll go take a look."

With the children thoroughly engaged in their kite project, Kate slipped away to the bedroom.

Chapter Twenty-Four

When Kate finished reading Wyn's letter, she carried the envelope into the living room. Now she'd have to tell the children that she'd located their father. To withhold all the love he conveyed in the letter for even one day would be a crime against Wyn as well as his children. The knowledge that their father loved them far outweighed the possibility that they might be disappointed later.

"I need to interrupt your kite building for a minute or two," she said.

They all looked up from their work. Megan must have caught the tremor in Kate's voice because she frowned. She was a very intuitive young lady.

"Is something wrong?" Megan asked.

"Not exactly, but I do have something important to share with you." She had all their attention now.

"Something about Ma?" Gwen asked.

"No, your father. I finally located him. I met and talked to him last week."

"Is he all right?" Megan asked.

"Is he gonna come get us?" Beck looked torn between wanting to know the answer and fearing what that answer would be.

"He's in Turney Center Industrial Prison near Nashville. He's written you all a letter. I hope you don't mind that I read it first. I wanted to be sure . . ." Letting the thought trail off, she held up the envelope for them to see. "I think it would work best if you sit together on the couch and Megan reads the letter out loud."

Hesitantly, Megan stood and took the envelope from Kate. She removed the three sheets of lined paper, unfolded them, and glanced at the message carefully printed in a bold hand.

"Come on, guys. Let's see what Pa has to say."

Her siblings followed her to the couch, plopping down on each side of Megan as though she was planning to read them a bedtime story.

As Megan smoothed the paper flat, Kate joined Paul and slipped her arm around his waist. He hooked his arm around her shoulders, giving her a reassuring hug.

Megan began to read out loud. "Dear Megan, Gwen, and Beck. I know you probably can't remember me, but there hasn't been a day that has gone by that I haven't thought of you and missed you and wished that I could be with you.

"I'm sorry that your Ma died. I know you must miss her a lot. I'm sure she always tried to do right by you and raise you as best she could. She loved you very much."

As she listened to the letter, Kate rested her head on

Paul's shoulder. The children were riveted by their father's words, particularly when he spoke of his feelings when each of them had been born and how he'd held them and counted their little fingers and toes.

Tears streamed down Kate's cheeks, and she noticed Beck wiping away his own tears with the back of his hand. How dear these children had become in Kate's life. How much she hoped they would soon be reunited with their father.

Megan turned to the last page of the letter. "I don't know when I'll be able to see you, but I hope it will be soon. Until then, know that I love each of you with all my heart. Love, Pa."

Only the sound of Megan folding the letter and returning it to the envelope broke the emotion-laden silence in the room.

Megan lifted her head. "Can kids visit their dads in prison?"

Kate had to force air past the constriction in her throat in order to speak. "Yes. They have visiting hours on weekends. It might take a while to make the arrangements to visit him."

The guard at the gate had said it could take as much as thirty days to get the warden's approval. Kate prayed that wouldn't be necessary and that Wyn would be released before then. Unfortunately, the parole board making an exception to give Wyn a compassionate early release seemed like a long shot.

"I could take him my kite and show him how good it flies," Beck said.

Megan elbowed her brother. "They won't let you fly a kite in prison."

The boy thrust out his chin. "Pa could ask."

In spite of herself, Kate laughed. "Why don't we take pictures of all of you flying your kites on Saturday? We can send the snapshots to your father. I think he'd like that."

That seemed to mollify Beck for the moment.

After a few more questions, Paul lured the children back to the dining table and their kites, and Kate went into her studio. She hadn't produced much in the way of stained-glass pieces for Steve Smith's craft booth at the Old Timer's Day affair.

Pulling her chair up to her drawing table, she contemplated the design she wanted to create for one of the sun catchers. She closed her eyes, picturing a column of sunlight illuminating a log cabin in the woods, smoke drifting up from a rock chimney, and a sense that the Lord was looking down on those who lived there.

Yes, that would do nicely.

She started sketching the design and had been at it for only a few minutes when the house phone rang. She let Paul answer it in the kitchen.

A moment later he appeared at her studio door. "Renee's on the phone. She's pretty hysterical. You'd better take it in the bedroom."

His worried expression and the tone of his voice propelled Kate to her feet. She hurried into the master bedroom and picked up the portable phone.

"What's wrong, Renee?"

"That *horrible* woman is going to take the children away," Renee wailed. "You have to stop her, Kate. You have to find some way to stop her!"

Kate didn't understand what she was talking about. "What woman?"

"That social worker lady, Valerie Hyland, that's who."

"Tell me exactly what happened. What did Ms. Hyland say?"

"She came over shortly after I got home from dropping off those sweet little children with Paul. She told me that because of those awful kidnappers, the children were no longer safe living in Copper Mill."

"That's ridiculous." The social worker's statement outraged Kate. "The kidnappers are in jail. The children aren't at any risk now."

"I tried to tell her that, but she wouldn't listen. She's going to send Megan to a group home in Chattanooga. The others will be moved to a home in Pine Ridge."

"Oh no . . ." Kate sat down heavily on the bed. "When is she going to move the children?"

"My mother and I both begged and pleaded to let them stay at least through Old Timer's Day. She finally agreed to wait until Saturday. She'll pick them up here at six o'clock. Kate, you have to do something to stop that woman."

"Yes, I know. But what? I'm trying to help their father get his parole. Unless a miracle happens, he can't possibly get parole for at least thirty days. Couldn't she wait that long? Leave the children with you until we know if Wyn's going to be released?"

"She seemed so adamant, Kate. You'll have to talk to her. I simply didn't know what else to say."

For a long while after Kate hung up the phone, she sat on the bed, her head in her hands, trying to think of a way to delay what now seemed inevitable. No grand plan or revelation came to her.

FIRST THING THE NEXT MORNING, Kate called Valerie Hyland. The woman was as unmoved by Kate's pleas as she had been by Renee's.

Kate talked to Hyland's supervisor, but the woman made it quite clear that she'd stand behind Hyland's decision. When Kate finally reached the Director of Children's Services, his answer was the same. For the children's safety, they would be removed from the loving home they'd found with Renee and placed with strangers.

Kate felt like crying over the miscarriage of justice that she couldn't prevent.

KATE WAS ON THE ROAD early Thursday morning en route to the Turney Center Industrial Prison for Wyn Carew's parole hearing. In her slender briefcase, she carried the notarized papers to substantiate Wyn's release plan. In her heart, she carried hope and a whole lot of prayers from Faith Briar's prayer circle.

The prison with its guard towers and razor wire looked no less intimidating than it had the first time she'd visited. The grim surroundings still gave Kate the unsettled feeling that once inside, a person might never come out.

Deacon Moore greeted her with his broad gold-tooth smile and booming voice. "Mrs. Hanlon, good to see you again." When she extended her hand, he took it in both of his. "Wyn's been a nervous wreck since you were here last week."

"I confess I'm a little nervous myself."

"Everyone is at a parole hearing. All you have to do is present Wyn's release plan to the hearing officer as thoroughly as you can. He'll probably ask you some questions, which I'm sure you'll be able to handle. He'll be asking questions of both Wyn and myself as well. Then it will all be left up to the hearing officer's recommendation and the parole board."

"I'm rather hoping the Lord will have a hand in whatever the decision is."

Deacon laughed a deep rolling sound. "Amen to that, sister."

As they waited, Kate told Deacon about the social worker's plan for Wyn's children, the urgency of getting Wyn released so he could take custody instead of the state.

When she finished, Deacon said, "The Lord surely has his work cut out for him, doesn't he?"

"I don't often pray for a miracle, but I think that's what it's going to take this time."

Finally a guard announced Wyn's hearing.

Kate filed into a barren room with two metal conference tables facing each other. Wearing his prison garb, Wyn stood at the nearest table. Across from him was the hearing officer, a pale-faced, portly man in his fifties with a double chin and thinning hair. A stack of files balanced the table on either side of him. In between, a nameplate read August Huhn.

Kate forced a smile, acknowledging the hearing officer with a nod.

Wyn held out a chair for her. As he seated her, he whispered, "Did the kids get my letter?"

"Yes, they were so glad to hear from you. They want to come visit as soon as they can."

August Huhn slapped his gavel on the table. "Let's get on with it, folks." He whipped open the file folder in front of him.

Moving away from Kate, Wyn seated himself in the middle, with Deacon on his left. Kate removed the notarized papers from her briefcase and placed them on the table. The uniformed guard who'd admitted them to the hearing room remained standing behind them, guarding the door.

Mr. Huhn rattled off case numbers, reason for incarceration, and other pertinent information before turning to Wyn, his tone sarcastic.

"All right, Mr. Carew, tell me why the good people of Tennessee should allow a fellow like you back into their midst."

Wyn cleared his throat. "My children need me, sir. Their mother died recently, and they don't have any other family. Mrs. Hanlon here, she's a preacher's wife, she's been looking out for them. I'd like a chance to do that myself."

"Everybody's got a sad story today," Huhn grumped. "So tell me, what's your release plan?"

Kate spoke up. Step-by-step, she told the hearing officer about the arrangements she'd made for Wyn's employment, a place to live, and supervision while he was on probation. When she finished, she handed the paperwork to the guard, who carried it to Huhn.

He flipped through them quickly, then looked up. "Anything else you want to say, Mrs. Hanlon?"

"Yes, sir. In order to keep the family intact, Mr. Carew

needs to be released by this weekend. Therefore, I'd like to request that the parole board grant Mr. Carew a compassionate early release no later than this Saturday."

Huhn squinted across the room at her. "You've got to be kidding. A compassionate early release? Never heard of such a thing."

"Sir, I've been informed by Children's Services that Mr. Carew's three children will be separated and placed in different foster homes, the oldest girl in a group home."

Kate heard Wyn suck in a shocked breath, but he held his tongue.

"They are to be removed from their current setting by six o'clock Saturday. I'm concerned about the long-term harm this separation, on top of their mother's recent death, will do to the children. I'm hoping you'll agree that Mr. Carew has earned his parole through his hard work, and that the interests of the state of Tennessee and its people are best served by keeping his family intact."

Silently, Huhn smoothed his palm over his thinning hair. Beads of sweat had begun to form on his forehead. "What do you have to say, Deacon Moore?"

"I believe Wyn Carew is repentant and has prepared himself well for his release and his life outside of prison. Given the circumstances of his children, I echo Mrs. Hanlon's request for a compassionate early release for Mr. Carew."

"*Hunh*. The parole board meets on Saturday." The hearing officer stared at them for a few seconds, then pounded the table with his gavel again. "This hearing is closed. The prisoner is to be returned to his cell, and the civilians escorted out. Good day."

Stunned by the sudden and inconclusive end of the hearing, Kate was ushered out of the room along with Deacon Moore.

"It's all in the Lord's hands now," he said as he told her good-bye.

Kate could only hope the Lord had a miracle planned.

Chapter Twenty-Five

Paul left the house early Saturday morning to help set up the booths for Old Timer's Day on the Town Green.

In the kitchen, Kate pulled a big mixing bowl from the cupboard and the pans she needed for the double batch of brownies she'd decided to contribute to the Faith Freezer booth.

The act of melting unsweetened chocolate and shortening together reminded her of the way two rivers came converged, at first separate and then flowing as one. She and Paul had joined in a single river of life and love many years before, in time bringing their children into the current that carried them along God's path.

Not all families were as fortunate, she realized. For whatever reason, the Maddock family had been caught in unfriendly eddies. Fear gripped her as she thought of the children being separated and Wyn being denied his parole. What tributary would they all follow if the worst happened?

Sifting the flour and a cup of sugar with baking powder and salt, she considered the ingredients that made for a happy family. Even without their mother, she believed with all her heart that Wyn could create that kind of family with his children, given the chance.

As she mixed the nuts into the dry ingredients, she acknowledged that the course of any family could hit some rough spots. A stubborn faith in the Lord had always helped her get past those moments.

Trying to shake off her melancholy mood, she finished mixing the ingredients together and poured half of the batter into each of two greased pans, then slipped the pans into the oven. While the brownies baked, she dressed, then loaded her meager contribution of stained-glass pieces for Steve Smith's Appalachian craft booth into the car. When the brownies had cooled, she cut them into squares and packaged them for the booth.

There'd been no word from Deacon Moore about Wyn's parole hearing, and her spirits were low as she drove into town.

Fearing the worst, the previous evening Kate had put together packets of writing paper and stamped envelopes she addressed to herself. She'd give those to the Maddock children so they could let her know their new addresses. Ms. Hyland, she was sure, wouldn't be willing to provide that information.

Although the day's events weren't fully under way yet, there were dozens of people milling around on the Town Green. Many of the locals, including Kate, wore old-fashioned dresses, and the men had donned overalls and straw hats to help carry out the theme.

Colorful booths had been erected around the periphery of

the green, with balloons attached that swayed gently in the morning breeze.

Kate delivered her brownies to the Faith Freezer booth first. Several cakes had already arrived, as well as trays of cookies.

"Looks like we're going to have a successful bake sale," she commented to Millie Lovelace and Dot Bagley, who had volunteered for the first shift of the day.

"It will be if Dot isn't tempted to snitch too many cookies while no one is looking." Millie appeared ready to keep careful track of the booth's inventory of cookies and cakes and make sure no one made off with any merchandise without paying.

Dot laughed, "I'm sure you'll save me from temptation, Millie. But you have to admit, Kate's double-chocolate brownies are hard to resist."

Not wanting to get in the middle of Millie's snit, Kate excused herself, promising she'd be back for the afternoon shift. She retrieved her stained-glass pieces from the car and carried them to the craft booth.

Dressed in a turn-of-the-century merchant costume, a long black jacket, and a frilly white shirt with a string tie, Steve Smith was setting out displays of wooden tops, old-fashioned spin toys, hardwood yo-yos, hand-woven wool shawls, monoprint cards, baskets, and ceramics. At the back of the booth, Steve had hung two lovely handmade quilts.

"Goodness, Steve, what a wonderful assortment of crafts," Kate said.

He smiled shyly. "We have a lot of talented people living in Copper Mill."

Kate handed him her three meager pieces of stained glass. "I'm glad you didn't rely on me to fill up your booth. I'm afraid I've been too busy to get much work done in my studio."

"Yes, I heard about the diamond thieves you tracked down." He held up each sun catcher to the light before placing it on the display table. "These are quite nice, Kate. They'll be snapped up in no time."

Kate was far more concerned about the Maddock children than the sale of her sun catchers.

From halfway across the Town Green, Renee called to her and waved. "Yoo-hoo, Kate! Here we are." The older woman was tottering along on three-inch heels, carrying Megan's colorful kite. Kisses bounced along in his tote, slung over Renee's arm.

Megan, who had a cardboard box in her arms, trudged along behind Renee, and Gwen and Beck followed behind with their kites. The children's heads were down, their shoulders slumped in obvious misery. They were fully aware that this was their last day in Copper Mill.

The thought of the children leaving, of them being separated from one another, made Kate almost physically ill. She forced a happy smile.

"Good morning! Did you bring your cornhusk dolls?" she asked Megan.

Megan's silent shrug spoke volumes about her state of mind as she handed the box to Kate.

"Oh, let me take a look."

Placing the box gingerly on the display counter, Kate examined Megan's work. The diamond necklace on the old-fashioned doll had been replaced with bits of stained glass.

Megan had also created a horse with a rider on his back, a kneeling boy playing marbles, and a guitar-playing cowboy.

"These are wonderful, Megan. You're very talented."

"For all the good it does." The young adolescent, in obvious pain, studied the ground as though hoping a hole would open up and swallow her.

Kate lifted Megan's chin. "You *are* talented and good and kind and smart. I'm very proud of you. Wherever you go, you remember that."

Tears glistened in Megan's eyes. "Yes, ma'am."

Steve took the dolls out of the box, raving over each one and placing them in a prominent position on his counter. He arranged to pay Megan her share of the proceeds at the end of the day before she left for Chattanooga. Nothing he said, however, seemed to cheer Megan or her siblings.

In the middle of the green, Skip Spencer was beginning to organize games for the children. He used an electric bullhorn to announce the events. First up was a three-legged race.

With the promise of an ice-cream cone, Paul managed to lure Beck into being his partner for the race. The young man who'd been so taken with Megan at the SuperMart invited her to join in the fun. Kate and Gwen became partners for what turned out to be a failed but hilarious effort in the women's division of the race.

By late afternoon, the children were into the spirit of the day, joining in the water-balloon toss and the hoop-rolling race. It didn't matter whether or not they won. They were having a wonderful day. But Kate knew their time left in Copper Mill was ticking away as surely as the sun followed its ordained path into the western sky.

The next event was the kite-decoration-and-flying contest.

Watching from the Faith Freezer booth, Kate looked across the expanse of the Town Green. She squinted, spotting a large black man ambling toward her. For a moment, she thought—

"Deacon Moore!" Leaving the booth in Livvy's capable hands, Kate hurried to meet Deacon and the man walking beside the chaplain, Wyn Carew. He'd shed his prison garb and was dressed in khaki slacks and a sport shirt.

"Afternoon, Mrs. Hanlon," Deacon said, grinning broadly. "I brought you your miracle."

Kate practically leaped into the chaplain's arms to hug him. "How did you do it? How did you get Wyn out so fast?"

Chuckling, Deacon lifted her off her feet and hugged her back. "Wasn't my doing. Seems the Lord sent us the perfect hearing officer. August Huhn was raised in foster homes and hated it. He didn't want the same thing to happen to those little children you told him about. The parole board acted this morning."

Thank you, Lord!

She turned to Wyn, hesitated a moment, then hugged him too. "You're just in time for the kite-flying contest. Beck will be so excited you're here. All the children will be."

"I can't thank you enough, Mrs. Hanlon—"

"Seeing you and your children reunited is all the thanks I'll ever need."

She hooked her arm through Wyn's, ushering him toward the cluster of youngsters gathered around Skip with their kites. Paul was in the group as well.

"Paul!" she called, getting her husband's attention. She

mouthed the words, "Bring the children," and gestured to Wyn.

Paul caught on right away.

"I'm kind of nervous about meeting the kids," Wyn admitted.

"Don't be." Kate patted his arm. "They're your family."

Over the youngsters' objections, Paul pulled them away from the crowd and headed them, feet dragging, toward Kate.

It was Megan who recognized Wyn first. Her eyes widened. Her pace increased until she was almost running.

"Pa!" Sobbing, she flew into her father's arms.

Trying futilely to stanch the flow of her own tears, Kate stepped back out of the way to give the children room to meet their father.

Gwen and Beck approached Wyn more warily than their big sister had. In order not to tower over them, Wyn crouched down.

"How did you guys get so big?" he asked.

"I'm almost ten," Beck proudly said.

"Yeah, I know. But last time I saw you, you were only that big." He held his hands about a foot apart. "I've missed you so much. I thought I'd lost you . . ." His voice broke, and he started to cry.

Gwen stepped up. "Don't cry, Pa. You found us. It'll be okay now."

Given all the hugging and crying, those attending Old Timer's Day began to realize what was happening. They formed a protective circle around the reunited family, everyone smiling and some shedding their own tears.

Sheriff Roberts made his way through the crowd to Kate. "Looks like Mr. Carew got here in time for the big news."

Puzzled, Kate asked, "What news?"

"The insurance company for the jewelry store in Knoxville called me. There's a reward for the return of the stolen diamonds. They wanted to know who to make the check out to. It's pretty substantial."

He named an amount that made Kate's jaw drop. That money could be put to use for any number of good causes. But Kate knew exactly where the Lord intended it to go.

"Have them make out the check to Wyn Carew. He's going to need it to help put his family back on their feet."

Sheriff Roberts shoved his hat back farther on his head and smiled. "I figured that's what you'd say. I'll let them know."

Apparently, Skip Spencer was anxious to get on with the kite-flying contest and used his bullhorn to announce that fact.

"Pa, can you help me fly my kite?" Beck asked.

"Me too," Gwen echoed.

"I sure can. In fact, I bet we can fly your kites up so high, your ma will be able to see them from up in heaven."

"Maybe we can write her a note and send it up with the kite," Gwen suggested. "She'd want to know you came and got us."

Taken aback by Gwen's request, Wyn looked around for some help. "I don't know if . . ."

"That'll work," Paul said. "I'll get some paper, the kids can each write a quick note, and we'll attach them to the kite strings."

When the notes were ready, Paul made some last-minute adjustments of the string and attached the children's messages.

Meanwhile, dozens of children spread out across the green, trying to give one another enough room so their kites wouldn't tangle together. The afternoon breeze wasn't very strong. The heavier kites tended to lose their lift early and crash to the ground. A few kites headed directly for the trees at the far end of the green and got snared in their branches.

Kate held her breath as Wyn coached each of his children in turn. He gave the kites a running start, then hurried back to the kids to make sure their brightly colored kites continued to rise and catch the stronger gusts above the treetops.

Attached to the strings, the squares of white on which the children had written notes to their mother grew smaller and smaller as the three kites raced skyward.

Struck with gratitude for the Lord's blessings on this family, Kate recalled Matthew 19:14, where Jesus said, "Let the little children come to me, and do not hinder them, for the kingdom of heaven belongs to such as these."

Taking Paul's hand, she continued to watch the flight of the kites and said a silent *Amen*.

About the Author

CHARLOTTE CARTER has authored more than forty novels and many nonfiction books. She has received various awards, including the prestigious National Reader's Choice Award and the Career Achievement Award by *Romantic Times* magazine. Charlotte and her husband live in Southern California, and have two daughters and five grandchildren.

A Note from the Editors

THIS ORIGINAL BOOK was created by the Books and Inspirational Media Division of Guideposts, the world's leading inspirational publisher. Founded in 1945 by Dr. Norman Vincent Peale and Ruth Stafford Peale, Guideposts helps people from all walks of life achieve their maximum personal and spiritual potential. Guideposts is committed to communicating positive, faith-filled principles for people everywhere to use in successful daily living.

Our publications include award-winning magazines such as *Guideposts* and *Angels on Earth*, best-selling books, and outreach services that demonstrate what can happen when faith and positive thinking are applied in day-to-day life.

For more information, visit us at www.guideposts.com, call (800) 431-2344 or write Guideposts, PO Box 5815, Harlan, Iowa 51593.